SUDDENLY YOURS

A SWEET BILLIONAIRE ROM-COM

CELEBRITY LOVE IN NEW ORLEANS
BOOK 3

KATIE TALBOT

LAKE VISTA
PRESS

Cover design by Beck and Dot Book Covers

Published by Lake Vista Press

978-1-969144-06-6 (ebook)

978-1-969144-07-3 (paperback)

First edition, 2026

For my parents, who always fostered my love of reading and writing.

1

"Lady, you've got about one minute before I have a full-blown panic attack."

I glanced in my rearview mirror at the woman behind me—Ms. Last-Minute, as I'd already dubbed her. Every airport shuttle has one: the passenger who tries to squeeze in one last errand before heading to the airport and then expects me to pull a miracle in traffic. She kept glaring at her watch.

Seated beside her was her polar opposite: Mr. Five-Hours-Early. He'd been checking his laminated itinerary since we pulled out of the French Quarter. Tall, thin, glasses perched on the tip of his nose, he looked like a librarian who'd just discovered someone returned a book with notes in the margins. In pen.

If stress had a buddy-cop movie, it would be these two.

"You're both going to make your flights," I said, easing into the exit lane. "Sir, you'll have plenty of time to rewrite your keynote for that academic conference in New York, and maybe even find a way to sneak in a Lord of the Rings quote. And ma'am, you'll get to your gate with three whole minutes to spare. Just enough time to get the coffee stain out of your blazer so you can crush that big Dallas pitch to the regional sales team."

Mr. Five-Hours-Early sighed and slid his itinerary into a leather folder with surgeon-level precision. "Kathleen," he said, adjusting his glasses, "you're probably right. Worrying never helps. Except when your panel's up against the free lunch."

Ms. Last-Minute glanced at me in the mirror and gave the tiniest, still-panicking-but-trying smile. "Thanks, Kathleen," she said.

As we pulled up to the terminal, I hit the button to open the doors. "Alright, folks. If you start to feel anxious at the gate, just give me a call. Here's my number." I scribbled it on a couple of pieces of paper. "Have a safe trip and may all your overhead bins be empty."

Ms. Last-Minute slid a five into my tip jar. "Thank you. You too."

I wasn't going anywhere—but sure. Me too.

Mr. Five-Hours-Early surprised me. Just before stepping off, he turned back and handed me a twenty. "This is for you," he said, smiling. "Thanks for helping calm me down. A little kindness goes a long way."

I tucked it into the jar and gave him a salute. "So does caffeine. Good luck out there."

As they hustled toward the entrance, I felt a small surge of pride. Driving a shuttle to the New Orleans airport wasn't exactly my dream job, but it paid the bills, came with housing, and gave me a chance to chip away at my debt. Plus, I enjoyed calming down stressed travelers. There was something satisfying about turning someone's chaotic morning into a manageable one.

But I was relieved that my eight-hour day, which started at 4 a.m., was almost over. Another shift down, another small step toward getting out of debt. But just as I was about to pull away to drive the shuttle van back to headquarters, it happened.

Crunch.

The unmistakable sound of metal meeting metal. I glanced out the window and saw a sleek black limo very intimately acquainted with the front end of my shuttle. Great. Just what I needed at the end of my workday. My heart sank as I threw the van into park and stepped out, a dull ache settling in my chest. What a mess. This would extend my day by a few more hours with mountains of paperwork.

The limo driver was the first to emerge. He was an older man with silver hair. Slowly, he unfolded a walker from the front seat and took his time navigating around the limo, inspecting the back bumper. "Would you look at this?"

But something tugged at the back of my mind. His posture wasn't hunched in the way people who truly rely on walkers moved. His grip on it was light, almost casual. And when he bent to examine the fender, his knees flexed with ease. There was no strain, no hesitation.

Weird. Maybe adrenaline made you flexible?

Or maybe I was imagining things.

Just then, the back door of the limo swung open. Dressed in a tailored suit that looked like it cost more than my yearly salary, the passenger stepped out, wearing the kind of expression that could only be described as "seriously annoyed." His thick brown hair was perfectly tousled, as if he'd just stepped off a movie set rather than out of a wrecked limo. His eyes—dark, intense, and now locked on me—radiated the unmistakable look of someone whose day had just gone from bad to worse.

As he approached, I could feel his gaze sweep over me, taking in my windblown hair and the grease smudge on my cheek. Normally, I'd have my long blonde hair pulled back neatly, but this morning had been a mad rush, and now I was wishing I'd taken those extra thirty seconds. He was definitely not the kind of guy who appreciated the "just rolled out of bed" look.

Limo Guy brushed past the driver, who was still steadying himself on his walker. "I don't have time to wait around for the cops," he snapped. "I've got an important appointment downtown."

Important appointment? Of course, he did. Probably to pick up another three-piece suit or scold an intern for not polishing his shoes correctly. The driver, still calm, looked at him apologetically. "Sir, we can call another vehicle from the company, but it's going to take a bit to get through the traffic."

Limo Guy, visibly irritated, shook his head and yanked out his phone. As he pulled four sleek, designer bags from the trunk—because of course he had four—he barked into his cell phone, "I need a driver around the clock. Honestly, I should've had a helicopter waiting. This is inefficient!"

Oooh, somebody's getting fired for this, I thought, watching the poor guy on the other end of that call probably question every life choice that led to this moment.

The driver glanced at the mountain of luggage and then at me, his expression desperate. "I'm afraid I can't be much help, sir. But..." He turned to me. "Ma'am, could you possibly walk him to the parking garage? There's another limo waiting there. I'd do it myself, but as you can see..." He gestured to his walker.

I couldn't believe this was how my day was ending. "Sure, I'll help."

"Great," Limo Guy muttered, speed-walking toward the parking lot like someone had lit his designer shoes on fire. He had two bags. I grabbed the other two and hustled to catch up, my legs doing double time to match his runway-model stride.

"I'm Kathleen Avery," I said, slightly breathless but determined. He didn't answer. Didn't even glance my way. I just kept walking, as if I were invisible. Like I was just there to do his bidding.

Okay then. "Business or pleasure?"

"Neither."

"Cool, cool. Love a man of mystery," I chirped. "You should swing by the French Quarter. Grab some beignets, hear some music."

"I'm not in town to be a tourist."

Right. Of course not. Heaven forbid he should accidentally enjoy himself.

"Got it. A top-secret mission," I teased.

"Not really." His tone was flatter than a heart monitor.

I pressed on. "I once had a guy try to board a plane with a snake. Said it was his emotional support animal. Think you can top that?"

He shot me a look. "Why would I want to?"

Wow. Okay. "TSA didn't let him on, obviously."

"Good. That would've been a safety violation."

"Wow, you are a bucket of fun," I muttered.

"Look," he snapped, finally stopping. "I just need to get to the limo. Preferably without a full biography of every passenger you've ever driven."

"Sure," I snapped. "But just for the record, your limo backed into *me*."

He whirled around. "It backed into *you*?"

"You didn't feel it?" I said, incredulous.

He frowned. "Wait... I did feel something."

"Yeah. That was *my shuttle*. You hit *me*."

He paused, then waved a hand as if to dismiss me. "Whatever. Let's go."

Unbelievable. I stomped after him. "You know, I've had more stimulating conversations with Siri."

"Talk to her, then," he said, not missing a step. "She might actually care."

I clenched my teeth. "Seriously, what's your deal?"

"My deal is that I have to get to my appointment."

"Maybe if you weren't so busy being a jerk, you'd get where you're going faster."

He finally glanced at me. The look in his eyes was cold and arrogant. "Maybe if you knew how to drive, we wouldn't be in this mess."

My jaw dropped. "Excuse me? *You* hit *me*. You don't get to rewrite history just because you have an 'important appointment.'"

"Backup limo's waiting," he said, ignoring me again.

When we finally reached the sleek black vehicle, I *may* have dropped his bags with a little more enthusiasm than necessary. "Good luck at your very important meeting," I said, oozing sarcasm.

He didn't thank me. Just nodded and climbed inside.

As the limo disappeared into the distance, my irritation started to simmer. Who did that guy think he was? Snapping orders, his laser focus on whatever 'important' appointment he had, like nothing else mattered. *There's a whole city out there, pal!* I imagined saying to him. *Ever notice the way the sun hits the river in the morning? Or how people actually have lives that don't revolve around your calendar?* But no, Mr. Workaholic was too busy marching through life. Maybe if he pulled his head out of his spreadsheets for five minutes, he'd realize there's more to life than his next big deal.

Yet, as much as I wanted to stay mad, I found my eyes lingering on the spot where he'd stood, my mind betraying me with a little reminder of how good he looked in those perfectly tailored pants.

Ugh, why do the obnoxious ones always have to be easy on the eyes?

I shook my head. Nope. I knew his type. I used to *be* his type. Living for the next deadline, the next achievement, always chasing after something that didn't really matter in the end. No, thank you.

But as the limo disappeared around the corner, I couldn't stop thinking one very irritating thing: Heaven help me... he was hot.

With a quick shake of my head, I turned away from where the limo had disappeared and headed back to the scene of the accident. The limo and shuttle had both been pulled over to the side of the airport-access road, out of traffic.

The limo driver, who moments ago was barely moving with his walker, was now gesturing wildly at a cop, who was scribbling notes on his pad. The driver's frail act was gone—he looked like he'd just stepped out of a courtroom drama, pointing accusingly at my shuttle.

I barely had time to process that before I saw my boss, Jerry, standing next to them. Jerry was a short, stocky man with a permanent scowl etched on his face. His thinning hair was combed back in a way that made it look like he was trying to cover as much of his scalp as possible, and his eyes were narrowed, suggesting I was about to get the verbal equivalent of a slap upside the head.

"Kathleen!" he barked, his voice as gruff as sandpaper. "What the heck happened here? The limo driver says you plowed into him and then took off! Are you trying to get us sued?"

"What? No!" I protested, wide-eyed. "That's not what happened at all! The limo backed into me!"

The cop, a no-nonsense type with a stern expression, looked up from his notepad. "Miss, you left the scene of the accident. That's a serious offense. We're going with the limo driver's version."

I felt my stomach drop. "But it wasn't my fault! He backed into me. And I didn't leave; I was helping his passenger get to another limo."

Jerry threw his hands in the air, clearly not interested in excuses. "Helping his passenger? You should've stayed put! Now we're in deep trouble, thanks to you."

"Wait," I practically shouted. "The passenger can prove it!"

The cop raised an eyebrow. "And where's this passenger now?"

I looked around, my heart sinking. The limo driver, seeing my panic, smirked and jumped in. "Busy man, can't be reached. Looks like it's just your word against mine."

"But—"

The cop shook his head. "Sorry, miss, but that's how it's going to be. You shouldn't have left the scene, no matter the reason."

I felt my face flush with frustration. The limo driver looked smug, and I had to resist the urge to say something I'd regret.

Jerry shook his head, his scowl deepening. "You'd better hope this doesn't cost us, Kathleen, or you're going to be in a world of hurt."

I nodded, trying to keep my cool, but inside, I was fuming.

As soon as the cop and limo driver were out of earshot, Jerry turned to me, his grimace set in stone. "Kathleen, you're fired."

The words hit me like a ton of bricks. "What? You're going to fire me just for this? It's just a little fender bender!"

Jerry crossed his arms, his expression as unyielding as ever. "You abandoned the shuttle. That's negligence. And let's be honest, you talk too much. People don't need therapy when they're heading to the airport."

My rising frustration made it hard to keep my voice steady. "I just try to help people relax before their flights! Isn't that a good thing?"

Jerry wasn't having any of it. "That's not your job. Your job is to operate the shuttle and ensure everything runs smoothly. You failed at that."

My stomach flipped over, and the world tilted just a bit. *You failed.* The chorus of my life. But I didn't have room for failure at the moment. My debts, my future—it all depended on keeping a job. And this one paid well. I would not cry. But I could curse Mr. Workaholic. I hope whatever meeting he was racing to was worth it. May his PowerPoint crash and his latte be lukewarm.

"Kathleen! Kathleen!"

I looked up to see Mr. Five Hours Early jogging across the road, waving at me. He looked more jittery than ever. "Excuse me," he stammered, wringing his hands. "Could you... um... help me calm down? I, uh, get really anxious before flights, and you were so helpful earlier..."

I opened my mouth to respond with reassurances, but Jerry cut in with a dismissive wave. "We don't have time for this. You're on your own, pal."

I couldn't believe what I was hearing. *How could he be so heartless?* I turned to Jerry, my frustration boiling over into something much stronger. "You know what? No. I'm not going to let you treat people like this. Maybe people do need someone to talk to before they fly. That's what made this job worth doing!"

The nervous flyer's eyes darted between me and the terminal like he was trying to calculate the odds of survival. I stepped closer and gave him my calmest smile.

"Hey," I said. "You're okay. Your plane will be piloted by professionals who do this every day. Look, nearly *three million* people fly in and out of U.S. airports *every single day*. And around the world? We're talking almost *100,000 flights a day*. And you know what happens on most of them?"

I gestured towards the sky. "*Absolutely nothing.* Flying is actually the safest form of transportation. Statistically safer than driving."

I pointed behind me, where anyone could see the shuttle's dented bumper. "*Much* safer than driving."

He laughed—just a little.

I put my hand on his arm. "Take a deep breath, walk back in there, and think of it as your next big adventure. You've got my cell phone number. Call me if you need anything."

He hesitated for a second, then straightened up a little, a spark of determination flickering in his eyes. With a nod, he turned around and marched back into the airport, his carry-on wobbling behind him, but his steps a little more confident than before.

I glanced over at Jerry, who was staring at me like I'd just sprouted wings and started flapping around the airport. He didn't get it, but that was fine. What I'd done mattered, even if Jerry never realized that. His expression hardened into his familiar scowl. "Well, congratulations, Kathleen," he spat. "Now, not only are you fired, but you lose the apartment too. I was going to let you stay another month, but not anymore."

The world seemed to tilt. *The apartment too?* My heart pounded as the reality of my situation crashed over me like a tidal wave. This wasn't just a setback—this was my life unraveling. I didn't have a family I could fall back on, nor was there a cushy inheritance waiting to bail me out. Losing my job was bad enough, but losing my apartment was even worse. That was everything. *Where was I supposed to go?* The walls seemed to close in around me, suffocating in their finality. I had nowhere to turn, no safety net to catch me as I fell. This wasn't just a bad day; this was the kind of disaster that could screw up my entire life.

As if to add insult to injury, my phone buzzed. I glanced down to see a text from Ms. Last-Minute: "Thank you so much. I made my flight!" Along with it, a selfie of her grinning on the plane like she'd just won the lottery. I held up my phone. "My passenger made her flight."

Jerry looked at me like I'd given away the nuclear codes. "You gave her your number?"

I shrugged. "What, you don't exchange numbers with your airport shuttle driver?"

I stared at the screen. *At least someone's day turned out okay.* But Ms. Last Minute's relief only amplified my own sense of defeat. Everything I'd worked so hard to maintain was slipping away.

Jerry's voice cut through my thoughts like a knife. "You've got until the end of the week to get your stuff out of the apartment."

I swallowed hard, trying to keep the tears from spilling over. *Don't let him see you cry, Kathleen. You're stronger than this.* But deep down, I wasn't so sure. Losing the job was one thing, but losing the roof over my head? That was a new kind of desperation.

I took a shaky breath and nodded. "Fine." I hoped my voice didn't betray the chaos inside. "I'll be out by Friday."

As I walked to the bus stop, I tried to focus on the silver lining. Sure, I'd just lost my job and my apartment in the span of ten minutes, but it wasn't all bad.

I still had Alex. A superhero in scrubs. A handsome doctor boyfriend—every woman's dream. Right then, all I wanted was to wrap myself in his arms and let him remind me that things would get better.

2

I FELT my spirits lift as the most gorgeous man I'd ever seen stepped out of a hospital room, looking effortlessly perfect in a doctor's coat. Alex Steele. Six feet of calm, dark blond perfection, with warm, hazel eyes that could make anyone feel at ease.

For a moment, I just stood across the hall from him, staring, hardly able to believe that someone like him was mine. It felt unreal —like I was living in a dream where I was dating the kind of man other women could only fantasize about.

He was always put together. Patients loved him, of course. Who wouldn't? He had a charm that made people trust him instantly, as if he were some kind of reassuring anchor in a stormy sea. And it wasn't just patients. Nurses, fellow doctors, even the administrative staff— they all seemed to light up when he was around. It wasn't just his looks or his skill; it was the way he carried himself, with confidence and ease.

I couldn't believe my luck. To be dating a guy like Alex, who had his life so perfectly together. He had never known hardship a day in his life. He'd started the race way ahead of the starting line, like life had handed him a head start while the rest of us were still tying our shoes. And honestly, there was something comforting about being with someone who'd never faced real struggles.

Sure, our conversations might not have been deep enough to solve world hunger, but with someone as incredible as Alex, who needed profound? Just being with him felt like an achievement.

Seeing him made the chaos of my morning feel like a distant memory.

I took a step forward and froze.

Another doctor stepped out from behind him. A stunning woman with glossy hair and a toothpaste-commercial smile. She placed her hand on my boyfriend's arm possessively.

I glanced at the sign on the door they'd just exited: "Supply Closet."

A weird, hot knot twisted in my stomach.

And then, I noticed Alex's doctor's coat.

It didn't fit him right. The seams were straining across his shoulders, as if they were begging for mercy. The sleeves barely grazed his wrists.

And stitched neatly on the pocket, just above his perfect chest: Dr. Elle Sparks.

I think I made a sound. A tiny, involuntary gasp or maybe a small, incredulous *"huh?"* Whatever it was, it got his attention because Alex finally noticed that I was there. And he didn't look happy to see me. Actually, he resembled a deer in headlights. He rushed across the hallway, grabbed my arm as if I were an unstable patient, and he ushered me into an empty room. The door clicked shut behind us.

"Kathleen," he said, voice tight, "what are you doing here?"

"I lost my job," I said, stepping toward him, arms open for a hug. For comfort. For *something*.

He blinked. "Again?"

That one word landed like a slap. No concern. No sympathy. Just pure, undiluted annoyance.

Before I could even flinch, he stepped back, creating the kind of distance usually reserved for contagious patients.

He tugged at the too-tight sleeves of the lab coat as if they were suffocating him (not as much as I was, apparently), and hit me with the kind of tone doctors use when telling you anesthesia isn't covered by your insurance: "We need to talk," he said. "I've fallen for someone else."

No warning. Just an emotional scalpel right to the chest.

And then—because apparently breaking my heart wasn't dramatic enough—he launched into *their* origin story.

"As crazy as it sounds, we were enemies," he began, with the kind of breathless sincerity usually reserved for reality TV confessionals. "Fierce rivals, both gunning for lead intern. Always neck and neck."

He paused, as if he expected me to faint at the romance of it all. I didn't.

"But fate had other plans. We got trapped in an elevator during a blackout—just the two of us, no way out. And then, an emergency hit. Right there. In that tiny, dimly lit box, we performed surgery together. Hands moving in perfect sync. No instruments, barely any light... but somehow, we saved a life."

He looked off, misty-eyed, like he was reliving a scene from *Grey's Anatomy*.

"That was the moment everything changed," he whispered.

I blinked. Was I supposed to swoon? Applaud? Offer to write the screenplay?

The whole thing felt surreal, like I'd been yanked out of my own breakup and dropped into a hospital-themed soap opera. But no. This wasn't fiction. This was my life. Unraveling in real time, beneath flickering fluorescent lights and the faint smell of antiseptic.

"You can't be surprised," he continued in that infuriatingly calm, doctor-y tone, like he was explaining a diagnosis to a particularly slow patient. "You and I have been dating for two years, and you've never really opened up to me. It's like there's this wall between us." He sighed, as if I was supposed to feel guilty for not burdening him with my baggage when he had to save lives every day.

My words failed me. I was still trying to wrap my head around the absurdity of the situation.

"I need someone with more drive," he went on, his voice slipping back into that condescending, I-know-what's-best-for-you tone. "Someone like you used to be in high school. You were valedictorian. You had so much ambition back then. Now, well, you're not that person anymore. You're wasting your potential, Kathleen."

My eyes narrowed, and I resisted the urge to laugh in his face, to blurt out that he hadn't even been in the top half of our high school class. I silently cursed the day I had decided to attend our high school reunion. *Who knew that one night of bad punch and awkward small talk would lead to this mess?*

He didn't seem to notice my growing discomfort. "Elle—Dr. Sparks—she's got that fire, that passion for medicine. She's everything I need in a partner."

Something struck me as he kept talking. Dr. Elle Sparks. The name sounded so familiar, but I couldn't quite place it at first. Then, like a ton of bricks, it hit me. Sparky. I had heard all about Sparky. Sparky was always doing something impressive. Sparky can intubate a patient in under thirty seconds, whatever that means. Sparky's the best at managing... um, intracranial something-or-other post-op. And Sparky could assist in a double-arterial bypass, just like she was flipping pancakes. Not that I had the slightest clue what a double-arterial bypass actually involved, but judging by the reverent way Alex said it, it might as well have been open-heart brain surgery on a moving train.

I blinked, the pieces falling into place. He had been talking about Sparky our entire relationship. Sparky was the superstar, the one who could handle any medical crisis without breaking a sweat. Somehow, in my head, I'd always pictured Sparky as some rugged, middle-aged guy with a gray beard and a gruff voice—maybe because the way Alex talked about Sparky made it sound like he idolized him. Um, *her*.

So, Sparky wasn't a grizzled, experienced surgeon. Sparky was Dr.

Elle Sparks. And now, I was realizing that my boyfriend had been infatuated with her all along, right under my nose. All those times he'd gone on and on about Sparky's incredible skills and how Sparky had saved the day yet again, I'd thought it was just professional admiration.

I couldn't believe what I was hearing. Not only was he dumping me in the most cliché way possible, but he was doing it while wearing another woman's lab coat—a woman who had just stepped out of a supply closet with him. My life had officially become a bad soap opera, and I was stuck in the role of the blindsided girlfriend.

But he didn't have to know that.

"So, this is convenient," I said, trying to keep my voice steady and nonchalant, even though my insides were twisting.

He raised an eyebrow, clearly puzzled. "Convenient? Come again?"

"Yes, convenient," I repeated, forcing a smile that I hoped didn't look as strained as it felt. "Because, funny story, I was actually coming here to tell you that I've met someone too. And now that you're with Sparky, I guess I can finally be with him." I gave a slight shrug, like this was all perfectly casual. "So... I'm breaking up with you."

The words tumbled out. And as soon as I said them, a little pang of guilt twisted in my stomach. *Ugh.* I wasn't a liar. I wasn't the kind of person who cheated or played games or blurted out fake boyfriends just to save face. But standing there, still reeling from his elevator love story, I couldn't stop myself.

Alex squinted at me, clearly unconvinced. His brows lifted, skeptical and just a little smug. "You... met someone?"

And just like that, the guilt vanished. Poof. Replaced with pure anger.

Not that I would ever cheat on anyone, *ever*, but the way he looked at me, like I couldn't possibly have someone else interested in me?

No. Absolutely not.

Alex blinked, and for a split second, I thought I'd thrown him off balance. But then he looked at me with pity. "Right... Kathleen," he said, his tone as patronizing as a preschool teacher's explaining why we don't eat glue. He took my arm and walked me back into the hallway. "So, you'll be leaving now, then?"

"Of course," I replied, nodding enthusiastically. "I've got plans to see my new boyfriend."

"You do that," Alex said, with a look drenched in pity. "Your 'boyfriend,'" he added, complete with air quotes, like I was a mental patient who'd just invented an imaginary friend. *Oh, wait.*

Great, I thought, *now I'm the crazy lady who invented a boyfriend on the spot.*

I needed to get away from Alex, fast. When his back was turned, I dashed into what looked like another empty patient room. I leaned against the door, mentally kicking myself for thinking I could bluff my way through that disaster.

The room was dimly lit, casting long shadows across the walls. I quickly glanced around, and the room appeared to be deserted, but then I heard a noise. Something like the clacking of keys on a laptop. My heart skipped a beat as I peeked around the curtain.

Sitting in the hospital bed, typing furiously on a laptop, was none other than Mr. Workaholic from the airport. He looked just as grumpy as before, his brow furrowed in concentration.

I froze, my mind going blank with shock. Of all the people to run into here, why him? I could feel the heat rising in my cheeks as I scrambled to come up with a way to back out of the room without being noticed. *Just slip out quietly, no big deal.*

I took one slow, careful step backward—right into a metal tray stand. The clattering noise echoed through the room like a symphony of disaster. The tray skidded across the floor, clanging against the wall with a final, resounding bang.

Workaholic's head snapped up, his eyes locking onto mine. For a split second, neither of us moved.

I gave a sheepish grin. "Hey," I said, my voice a little too high-pitched. "Just, uh, passing through."

"*Passing* through?" he repeated, raising an eyebrow. "You mean *crashing* through?"

A jolt of panic shot through me. I should've turned around and left, but the words tumbled out of my mouth before I could stop them. "Thanks to you, I got fired." The moment the words left my lips, regret washed over me. *Why did I say that?* I never open up, never let anyone see what's really going on. And now, I've just thrown it all out there like it's no big deal. *What's wrong with me?* "Everything is going wrong in my life today."

Mr. Workaholic raised an eyebrow, unfazed. "Yeah, I could see that."

His casual acknowledgment stung, and something inside me snapped. "Oh, really? And how exactly could you see that?"

He shrugged, barely sparing me a second glance as his attention drifted back to his laptop. "Well, considering the way we met... Let's just say you didn't exactly strike me as someone who has it all together."

The casual way he said it, the way he barely even looked at me as he made that judgment, made my chest tighten with anger. It was like he had decided, from the very first moment, that I was some kind of disaster.

Maybe I was. But hearing it from him, in that cold, detached tone, made it feel so much worse. "Hey, mister, if you had stayed, I wouldn't have been fired. Your liar of a limo driver said I ran into him."

He sighed, not even glancing up from whatever he was working on, which was probably some critical spreadsheet that the world would end without. "It's unfortunate, but that's how the world works. You can't expect everyone to be honest."

The audacity of this man was unbelievable. Here I was, my life unraveling at the seams, and he had the nerve to sit there and lecture me like I was some incompetent child.

But of course, once I started, it was like the floodgates opened, and I couldn't stop. The words just kept tumbling out, each one more dramatic than the last. "I lost my job and my house and found out my boyfriend was cheating on me all in the same day. So thanks for asking. I'm doing just great! Really, I should start writing self-help books."

The heat of embarrassment crept up my neck. I never spill my guts to anyone, especially not to a jerk workaholic.

For a moment, just a split second, I thought I saw something soften in his eyes. But it was gone as quickly as it came, replaced by impenetrable coolness.

"It's Kathleen, right?" He didn't wait for me to respond, only put a hand on his chest. "Topher Brodie. Sorry to hear that things have been, uh, rough for you. But maybe this is an opportunity for you to reassess and focus on what's important. Like finding a new job."

I stared at him in disbelief. Was this his version of sympathy? "Wow, thanks for the heartfelt advice." My words dripped with sarcasm.

Mr. Workaholic, er, Topher Brodie, didn't rise to the bait, his fingers tapping away on his tablet. The sound grated on my already frayed nerves. I took a deep breath, trying to steady myself, and couldn't help but notice how sharp and put-together he looked in that suit. It fit his broad shoulders to perfection, and the pants emphasized his long, muscled legs, and—

Nope! I would *not* let this insufferable man distract me, no matter how hot he was.

I eyed him suspiciously. "What are you doing here anyway? You look like some kind of pharmaceutical sales rep or someone here to sell overpriced medical equipment."

He glanced up briefly, his expression unreadable. "Right now, I'm just handling some business."

"Did they hire you to scare patients into paying their bills on time or something?"

He shook his head, clearly uninterested in continuing the conversation. "Listen, I have a lot to get done. I'd appreciate it if you found somewhere else to process your issues."

I rolled my eyes, frustration bubbling up inside me. *Like I wanted to be stuck here with him, of all people.* I turned toward the door, ready to make my escape, but froze mid-step when, through the little window on the door, I caught sight of Alex outside, talking animatedly with Dr. Sparky. My stomach dropped. Oh, no. The last thing I needed was to run into them right now.

Without thinking, I ducked out of sight of the window, practically flattening myself against the wall like I was dodging laser beams in a spy movie. *Please don't see me. Please don't see me.*

Topher looked at me like I'd lost my mind. "What are you doing?"

I gave him a pointed look. "My ex-boyfriend is out there. With his new girlfriend. There's no way I'm walking out of this room right now."

Topher's annoyance was palpable. "Fine, then be quiet so I can get some work done."

"Fine," I slumped into the nearest chair. If he wanted silence, he was going to get the most passive-aggressive silence I could muster.

A minute passed before he spoke up again, his tone dripping with irritation. "I can hear you breathing."

I narrowed my eyes at him. "Oh, sorry. Let me just stop doing that for you."

He didn't respond, his attention already back on his screen. I crossed my arms and tried to make myself as small and invisible as possible. We fell into a tense silence. I hated him, or at least I wanted to. But sitting there, with the weight of the day pressing down on me, I realized just how alone I felt. And as much as I hated to admit it, his presence, however irritating, was the closest thing I had to comfort in this godforsaken hospital.

But I couldn't let him see that. No, I'd rather hold my breath until I pass out.

Sitting there, I avoided even glancing in Mr. Workaholic's direction, focusing on the wall instead. Alex's words echoed in my mind: how he said I never really let him in, not even after two years together. Maybe he was right, but a bitter sense of satisfaction washed over me. It was good, after all, that I never let anyone in. They always ended up proving you can't count on anyone but yourself. Alex and Mr. Workaholic were just reminders that opening up only leads to disappointment. Better to keep people at a distance, where they couldn't hurt me.

I leaned forward, resting my elbows on my knees, when suddenly, the chair wobbled. I tried to steady myself, but the chair leg must have been uneven because it tipped unexpectedly, and I found myself pitching forward. Instinctively, I reached out to grab something to stop my fall.

Unfortunately, that something was on the edge of the bed where Topher sat.

The next thing I knew, I tumbled onto the bed. There was no time to brace myself, no time to avoid what was coming next. I could only watch in horror as Topher, startled by the sudden movement, tried to sit up at the exact same moment.

Our heads collided with a dull thud, the impact sending a sharp jolt of pain through my skull. "Ouch!" I yelped, grabbing my forehead, while he let out a low grunt of pain, his eyes wide with shock. In the chaos, my legs got tangled in the sheets, trapping me against him. I could feel his hands instinctively grasping my arms as we both struggled to regain our balance, to pull ourselves out of this ridiculous mess.

But somehow, in the flurry of limbs and fabric, we ended up in a twisted, awkward heap, our faces inches apart, practically nose to nose. Time seemed to freeze, and for a second, I could only stare at him, wide-eyed and breathless.

Everything in the room disappeared—the hospital, the chair, the looming cloud of my own problems. All I could focus on was the warmth of his body pressed awkwardly against mine and the sheer embarrassment that made my cheeks burn like they were on fire. My heart hammered in my chest, a wild, erratic rhythm that only intensified the longer we stayed like that.

Just when I thought things couldn't possibly get worse, the door swung open.

Because of course it did.

A nurse walked in, her eyes going as wide as saucers as she took in the scene: the two of us, tangled in a mess of sheets.

"What on earth is going on in here?" she demanded, her voice dripping with the kind of disbelief usually reserved for catching teenagers making out behind the bleachers. "This is a hospital, not a motel!"

Topher sprang into action with the speed of someone who had just remembered an urgent meeting. We scrambled apart in a frantic rush, practically tripping over each other to untangle the sheets and put some distance between us. I managed to roll off the bed, landing in a heap on the floor with my pride barely intact, while he tried to straighten his suit like nothing out of the ordinary had happened.

I could still feel the heat in my cheeks as I desperately avoided looking at either of them.

The nurse shoved her hands on her hips. "Mr. Brodie, your mom needs you. You need to come now," she said, her tone all business. Then she glanced at me, eyebrows raised in judgment. "And your girlfriend can come too. Get yourselves in shape and head to room 5023 ASAP."

I blinked in surprise, processing the information that this work-obsessed, seemingly unflappable man had a mother in the hospital. A mother who needed him.

The empty room spun into another place and time, a different hospital room with beeps and yelling voices, with nurses pulling me away from the bedside.

Like those nurses, this nurse expected to be obeyed. She marched out without waiting for a response, leaving us standing there in stunned silence.

Topher shifted into action, his demeanor still sharp and focused, like nothing could throw him off. "There's a program running on my computer. The Wi-Fi in this place is terrible, and I can't risk moving the laptop, or I'll lose the connection."

His gaze landed on me with the same intensity he probably

reserved for boardrooms and deals. "I'll pay you five-hundred dollars to keep an eye on the laptop and bring it to room 5023 when the program's done."

I blinked, still trying to process the awkward collision, the nurse's orders, and now this unexpected request. He didn't waver, didn't show a hint of anything but confidence, like he fully expected me to agree without question. There was no room for vulnerability or uncertainty in his world.

He paused for a moment, then added, almost as an afterthought, "Just so you know, if anyone tries to steal the computer or mess with it, the security system will lock it down and wipe everything."

I didn't know what to say. Part of me wanted to tell him to shove his five-hundred dollars and that he should figure it out himself. But five-hundred dollars was more than just a little extra cash. It was enough to cover bills I'd been worrying about for weeks, enough to buy me some breathing room. I hesitated, suddenly aware of how much I needed that money. It was like a lifeline I couldn't afford to pass up. "Fine, I'll do it."

He gave a curt nod. "Just make sure it gets to room 5023 when the program's done running."

And with that, he turned and strode out of the room, as if it were just another day at the office.

I let out a sigh as the door clicked shut behind him.

So, let's recap: I'd lost my job, my home, and my boyfriend, and I was taking cash from a guy who probably had a personal assistant just to open his emails.

A guy who probably thought "roughing it" meant staying in a four-star hotel.

A guy who probably had a team to help him pick out his tie.

Really hitting new heights here. Yep, definitely living the dream.

3

I SAT BACK in the chair, the dull hum of Topher's laptop filling the room as I waited for his program to finish. Bored, I pulled out my phone. The moment I unlocked it, a notification popped up, and my stomach twisted into knots. My loan payment was coming due, and the app's warning flashed ominously in red. Great. Just what I needed.

With a sense of dread, I logged into my bank account, bracing for the worst. A negative balance glared back at me. I bit my lip, anxiety gnawing at my insides. I did some quick mental math. With the five hundred dollars I'd get from watching this laptop, I could barely scrape by and get my account back in the black. But that was just a Band-Aid, not a real solution. The looming sense of doom wasn't going anywhere.

I sighed, trying to shake off the worry and focus on the task at hand. The program on Topher's laptop was still running, lines of code or data, scrolling by on the screen. I had no idea what any of it meant, but it was clearly significant enough that Topher was willing to pay me to babysit it.

Finally, after what felt like an eternity, the program finished loading with a soft beep. I closed the laptop carefully, tucking it under my arm, and headed toward room 5023, where Topher's mother was.

As I approached, I heard voices. I stood outside the door and listened.

"Mom, it's probably nothing," Topher was saying. "Just some headaches."

"Topher, don't brush this off," replied a woman—I assume his mother—her voice laced with concern. "You've been working too hard, and stress can do terrible things to the body. You need to take care of yourself. What you need is a girlfriend, someone who'll look after you."

I leaned closer, trying to listen without getting caught.

"He does have a girlfriend," the nurse from earlier said, her voice chipper. "I walked in on him with a gorgeous girl downstairs."

I nearly choked. *Gorgeous? Was she talking about me? Wait, does she actually think I'm his girlfriend?* But before I could fully process that little bombshell, I heard Topher's panicked response.

"Girlfriend? That's... ha... No, she's..." He sounded like he was about to combust on the spot.

"Oh, Topher! This is wonderful news!" His mother's voice was practically bubbling with excitement. "I knew you'd find someone eventually. And she's here?! Right now?!"

"Mom, she's not—"

"Oh, don't be shy, dear! I want to hear everything!" his mother gushed, completely steamrolling over his attempts to clarify. *Great, now she's planning our imaginary wedding.*

"And she's not just beautiful," the nurse chimed in, because apparently, things weren't ridiculous enough already. "The way she looked at you, Topher, anyone could see the love in her eyes."

Love in my eyes? My face flushed with heat. *This is a nightmare. Please, someone, wake me up.*

"And what's her name?"

"It's Kathleen, but Mom, it's really not what you think—"

"Topher, it's as clear as day that she's important to you," the nurse said. "We're all just so happy to see how much she's brightened your mother's spirits."

"She's not my..." Topher's voice trailed off into a long pause. Then, almost like he was realizing it for the first time, I heard him say softly, "I haven't seen you this happy in a while, Mom."

As I strained to hear more, his mother's voice, warm and full of joy, broke the silence. "Oh, Topher, all I've ever wanted is to see you happy. And if she's the one bringing that smile to your face, then I already love her."

My face was practically on fire at this point. I leaned in a little closer, trying to catch every detail of this increasingly bizarre conversation.

Someone cleared their throat right behind me.

I froze, dread pooling in my stomach as I slowly turned around to see Alex standing there, glaring at me.

He leaned in, whispering through gritted teeth, "Kathleen, it's over between us. You have to go home. You can't stay here."

Alex's condescending tone made my skin prickle with irritation. My mind raced, searching for a believable excuse to salvage my dignity.

"I'm not here for you," I said, my voice a little too loud in my own ears. "I'm... I'm here for... my new boyfriend's mother!" I somehow managed not to wince. Inside the hospital room, Topher was trying to figure out how to convince his mother he didn't have a girlfriend, but out here, I was shamelessly using him and his mother to... what? Trick my ex into thinking I'm not pitiful? It was humiliating. And Topher would hate me even more than he already did if he knew. But he never would. We could stay right outside this room, nice and safe from any further awkwardness.

But just as I thought I might get away with it, the nurse pulled the door open, her eyes lighting up with recognition.

"Oh, is that Kathleen out there?" came the cheerful voice of

Topher's mother from inside the room, sending my stomach straight to the floor.

Great. Things just kept getting better.

The nurse stepped into the hall, eyes landing on me with far too much enthusiasm. "Yes! That's her! She's here with Dr. Steele."

I was not just drowning. Now, I was being actively dragged down by the weight of my own bad decisions.

Alex's smile faltered, and suddenly the nurse was waving me forward like a contestant on a game show. Before I could escape, I was ushered into the hospital room.

Topher's mother lit up the moment she saw me. "Oh, Kathleen! It's so wonderful to *finally* meet you!" she said, reaching for my hand like I was the answer to all her prayers. "Topher didn't tell me you were coming today!"

Of course he didn't. We'd met approximately three hours ago.

"Uh, yes, it's great to meet you too," I said, doing my best impression of a functioning adult while internally begging the linoleum to crack open and swallow me whole.

Then I felt Topher next to me, suddenly *very* close.

His voice was low, smooth, and pitched so only I could hear: "Play along."

I blinked at him. "What?"

He leaned in closer, giving me an awkward hug as he whispered in my ear. "That's your doctor ex over there, right? He looks ready to combust. My mom thinks you're my girlfriend. You want out of this alive? Don't blow it. And I won't either."

He pulled back, and I made eye contact with Alex. I didn't even like Topher. He was rude, smug, and entirely too good-looking for someone with that much attitude. But... Alex was watching.

And oh, he *did not* like what he was seeing.

Alex cleared his throat. "Wait. You're *Topher Brodie*. You own half of New York." His eyes bounced between me and Topher like he was trying to do the math and getting all the wrong answers. "You two are dating?"

Hold on. *Owns half of New York?* I looked again, suddenly clocking the designer shoes, the crisp shirt, the watch that probably cost more than my student loans.

Well. That explained the limo.

I caught the look on Alex's face—stunned, jealous, and a little desperate—and, honestly? That sealed it.

I felt Topher's hand brush against mine, and this time, I looped my arm through his.

To my surprise, he didn't flinch. He tightened his hold just slightly, like we'd rehearsed it.

"Yes, my boyfriend," I said, adding an extra scoop of saccharine to my voice and batting my lashes like I was auditioning for a Hallmark movie.

Topher's posture relaxed just a hair. He gave me the tiniest nod, almost like a thank you.

I leaned into him, aiming for graceful and effortless... and accidentally jabbed him in the ribs with my elbow.

Topher flinched, then subtly tried to shift away, but that only made it worse. My hair caught on one of his jacket buttons. Fantastic.

I winced, trying to untangle myself without yanking out a chunk of hair or blowing our cover. All while smiling like nothing was wrong.

Thankfully, no one seemed to notice our accidental slapstick routine. Alex and the nurse had turned their attention to Topher's mom, who was chatting away like this was the most heartwarming thing she'd ever seen.

Then, just when I thought things couldn't get weirder, Topher leaned in again, his voice warm and confident. "Honey, is that my laptop?"

Honey.

My heart did a little somersault.

I looked down at the laptop I'd been babysitting all morning and nodded, trying not to look like I'd just been tased. "Uh, yeah. Thought you might need it."

He smiled and gave my arm a squeeze that sent a jolt through my chest.

"Thanks, babe."

Babe. My heart zoomed again. At this rate, I'd need medical attention too.

As I was trying to process what was happening, my attention was pulled to Alex as he reached the door. He paused and turned back, his tone the confident, reassuring doctor that I knew so well. "Mrs. Brodie, Topher, I want you to know that the surgery that Dr. Julius is planning to remove the tumor is one he's performed many times, and I'm very confident it will be successful. You'll be home recovering in no time, just like we talked about."

Alex's eyes flicked back to me, narrowing with a suspicious look that seemed to linger. Topher must have sensed it, too, because he pulled me closer, tightening his grip around my shoulder in a gesture that felt both protective and possessive. Alex's jaw tightened ever so slightly, then he turned on his heel and left the room, the door closing behind him with a soft but decisive click.

Mrs. Brodie wasted no time. Her eyes sparkled with excitement. "So, how did you two meet? I'm dying to know the story."

Topher and I exchanged a quick, panicked glance, both of us scrambling for a story that made sense.

"At the airport," I blurted out just as Topher said, "In a car accident."

We quickly tried to recover.

"Actually, it was both!" My forced laughter felt strained. "We were at the airport, and, um, there was a bit of a fender bender in the drop-off zone."

"Yeah," Topher added, nodding. "She rear-ended my limo."

I whipped around to face him, my eyes narrowing. "Rear-ended? More like your driver backed into me!"

Topher raised an eyebrow, amusement flickering in his eyes. "Backed into you? You were practically parked in our blind spot, trying to squeeze into a space that didn't exist."

I smiled sweetly, but I wasn't about to let him off the hook. "Oh, please. Your driver was so focused on getting you to your next destination that he didn't even check his mirrors. He nearly turned my car into a speed bump!"

Topher leaned in slightly, his grin widening. "Well, maybe if you weren't so determined to snag a spot meant for a skateboard, you wouldn't have ended up nose-to-nose with my limo."

Mrs. Brodie watched our playful back-and-forth with a delighted smile. "And how long have you two been together?"

I glanced at Topher, trying to keep up the act while my mind raced. I've never been good at improv. "How long has it been, honey?"

Topher didn't miss a beat. "Six months," he said confidently, before adding with a wink, "though sometimes it feels like only a day."

I jumped in, smirking, "And other times, it feels like ten years."

Topher raised an eyebrow playfully. "Ten years? I was going to say a lifetime."

The nurse stepped in, her voice gentle but firm. "Alright, you two, time to let Mom get some rest. She's got surgery tomorrow, and after that, she'll need four weeks of recovery with absolutely no stress."

Mrs. Brodie reached out, her eyes glistening with tears. I walked over, and she grabbed both of my hands, her grip surprisingly strong, and pulled me into a hug. "Kathleen, I can't wait to get to know you better."

I was speechless, guilt thudding in my chest. This was all one big, elaborate lie, and yet here I was, playing along. Luckily, the curtain was about to drop on this ridiculous performance because the nurse shooed us toward the door. "Out you go. Let her rest."

We stepped into the hallway, and Topher leaned in close, his voice low. "We really need to work on our how-we-met story."

"Fine. We met while wrestling an alligator in the bayou." I rolled my eyes, crossing my arms defensively. "No, we don't have to work on our story. I'll take my five hundred dollars, thank you very much, and we can part ways." My tone was firm, hoping to make it crystal clear that this little charade had reached its expiration date. *Just take the money and run, Kathleen. No need to complicate things further.*

Topher took out his wallet and gave me the money.

"Nice doing business with you," I said, then started walking away.

He cleared his throat. "Just hear me out." I stopped and looked. His expression was completely serious, almost desperate. "Kathleen, my mom is so happy right now, and I haven't seen her like that in ages. Didn't you notice how she lit up? It's like she's finally got something to look forward to, something to keep her spirits up through all this. Please, just until after she's recovered from the surgery. Four weeks, that's all I'm asking."

I shook my head and walked outside and into the parking lot, Topher right beside me. "I'm not interested in being part of this soap opera. I'll take the five hundred bucks for babysitting your laptop, but that's it. I'm not signing up for a four-week charade."

But he didn't back down. If anything, he looked even more determined. "Kathleen, please. You don't understand. My mom hasn't been this happy in years. This whole thing has given her hope again. I've never seen her this excited about anything since she got sick. I can't take that away from her now."

"Topher." I sighed, trying to hold my ground. "I'm really sorry about your mom, but—"

"Please, Kathleen." He spoke softly, pleading. "I need to protect her, keep her spirits up. This might be the only way to do that. Just four weeks, that's all I'm asking. You don't even have to see me if you don't want to. You just lost your house, right? Stay at my place. It's a mansion in the Garden District. It's big enough that we'll never even have to cross paths. You don't have to pay rent, and you'll have time to find a new apartment. In return, my mom gets the peace of mind she needs. Please, I'm begging you."

I stared at him, feeling my resolve crumble. My mind flashed to my mounting debt, unpaid bills sitting on my kitchen counter, and the fact that I was one missed payment away from losing everything. I needed this more than I cared to admit.

I let out a long sigh, trying not to sound as defeated as I felt. "Look, I'm not an ogre. I'm not about to crush your mom's happiness."

His eyes snapped to mine, lit with a flicker of surprise, like he hadn't expected me to say yes, not even a little.

"So...?"

"Fine." I threw my hands in the air. "But only until she's better. And for the record, I'm not doing this for you. I'm doing it for her. And the free rent."

"Great," he said, pulling out his phone with zero hesitation, like he was checking off a task on a very long to-do list.

Just like that, the warmth he'd shown a moment earlier—the playful glances, the easy smile he'd flashed in front of his mom, the way he pulled me in when Alex was watching—gone. Replaced by the Topher I met at the airport: focused, cold, already swiping through emails like I was a line item on his calendar.

I gritted my teeth. "I'm not here to make your life easier, Topher."

"Yeah," he said without looking up. "I know. Believe me, I'm not expecting miracles. Just... don't mess this up."

There it was. The tone. Clinical. Detached. The same one he probably used to fire assistants and cancel meetings with people who had families and feelings. It made me want to scream.

Why was I doing this again? I hated his smug face. His total disregard for actual human emotion. And yet, I was saying yes. Because I didn't have a better option.

"Text me the address," I muttered, hating myself a little more with each syllable.

"I will," he said, already sliding into the backseat of a waiting town car. "I just need to take care of something first. I'll let you know where to bring your stuff."

Then the door shut, and he was gone.

I stood there for a second, blank. The bus wouldn't be there for an hour. So, with nowhere else to go, I wandered back into the air-conditioned lobby, collapsed into a plastic chair, and let out a groan.

Four weeks. Just four weeks of pretending to date a man who

thought manners were a scam invented by the weak. But at least I'd have a place to sleep. At least I wouldn't be checking my bank account and holding my breath every minute.

Twenty minutes crawled by. Each one gnawed at me with new doubts. This wasn't a real plan. It was only delaying the inevitable.

Movement snapped me out of it. Topher sprinted past me, his expression intense, as if the world might collapse if he didn't handle whatever task he'd set his sights on.

Without thinking, I shoved my phone into my bag and followed him, my heart pounding with a reluctant sense of obligation. Why was I doing this? I couldn't stand him, but somehow, there I was, trapped in a ridiculous situation. I caught up with him near the entrance. He looked pale.

"What's going on?" I asked.

He held up his phone. His voice cracked.

"I just got a 911 text about my mom."

4

I'D ONLY MET TOPHER that morning—barely enough time to form an opinion, though what little I'd seen hadn't been flattering. He was the kind of guy who barked orders and lived in a world of spreadsheets and endless meetings, a workaholic who seemed to think that was the only way to live.

But now I saw something else. Something I didn't expect.

He looked scared.

And I don't mean the 'forgot my password' kind of panic. This was on a whole different level.

It threw me. This was the same man who had barely glanced at me when we first met, as if I were just another minion to boss around. Now, his eyes were darting like he couldn't quite process what was happening.

He shoved his phone back into his pocket, his movements jerky. "Are you coming or not?" he asked, his voice tight but wavering just enough for me to catch it.

I hesitated for a heartbeat, then found myself saying, "Yeah, I'm coming." I didn't know this guy, but something in the way he looked, as if he was unraveling, made me want to help. I was his fake girlfriend, and aren't girlfriends—fake or not—supposed to do this kind of thing?

He turned and marched toward the hospital entrance, and I hurried to catch up.

Topher jabbed the elevator button repeatedly. "We should just take the stairs," he muttered, his voice sharp, as if the idea of waiting one more second for the elevator was physically painful.

If I hiked up five flights right now, I'd probably need a hospital bed myself. My calves were already screaming in protest at the thought.

Just then, the elevator doors slid open, and I nearly sighed in relief. *Thank you, universe.*

"My mother's so stubborn," Topher said, as the elevator jerked upward. "She wants to stay here, but I'm not taking any chances. I'll fly her to the finest hospital in the world, with the most renowned doctors on the planet. Whatever it takes."

I wasn't sure how to respond. I hardly knew this guy—just enough to realize he was the kind of person who tried to control everything around him, and right now, that control was slipping. "Maybe... let's just see what's happening first." I hoped my suggestion wouldn't set off another round of elevator-button-murdering.

But he hardly seemed to hear me. "This wouldn't be an issue if she were in New York. She could be near some of the world's top doctors, and I could be with her in minutes. I should've insisted on moving her closer to me. But no, she's too attached to this town."

I paused, unsure how far to push. "If she's attached, it means she's got a good life, one she enjoys, and that's important. That's something, right?"

Topher hesitated. "Yeah, she does love it here. You know, she owns Muses, that bar over in the Garden District."

My eyebrows shot up in surprise. "Wait, your mom owns Muses?"

"Yeah," he said, a little distracted, clearly still worried. "She's been concerned about leaving it in other people's hands while she's in the hospital, but I keep telling her she put a good group in charge. They've got it under control."

I blinked, processing that piece of news. Muses was one of the most popular bars in the city.

The elevator dinged, and the doors slid open to the fifth floor. Topher shot out like a man on a mission, his strides long and purposeful, while I scrambled to keep up.

When we reached his mother's door, he just stood there, the weight of what might be waiting inside clearly dragging him down.

Without really thinking, I reached out and touched his arm, a gesture that felt oddly intimate given how little I knew him. The warmth of his skin under my fingers sent a jolt through me, and I had to remind myself that this was just part of the act. Just me, trying to channel some of that comforting girlfriend energy I'd seen in the movies.

"Hey, whatever it is, you don't have to go through it alone." My voice was softer than I expected, as if I actually meant it. Which, weirdly enough, I did.

He looked at me then, really looked at me, and for a split second, I saw something flicker in his eyes. Surprise, maybe. My heart did an unexpected little flip.

Topher didn't say anything, just gave a short nod before pushing the door open. I followed him into the room, bracing myself for the worst. My mind had conjured up all sorts of grim possibilities, but none of them prepared me for what we saw.

There, in the center of the room, was Mrs. Brodie. She was perfectly fine and doing something I never would have expected.

She was propped up on the hospital bed, legs crossed under the blanket, and her attention was wholly on a stack of brightly colored magazines spread out on the tray table in front of her. She was meticulously cutting out pictures of cats, her tongue poking out slightly in concentration.

She held a bottle of glitter glue in one hand, carefully pasting the cut-out felines onto a large, pink construction paper card that read

"Get Well Soon, Doc!" in big, glittery letters. Now and then, she would pause to adjust her reading glasses, her expression a mix of determination and childlike glee as she decorated the card with stickers, sequins, and more glitter than should ever be allowed in a hospital room.

"Mom?" Topher's voice was a mix of confusion and disbelief, his earlier panic replaced with a kind of stunned shock. "What happened? What's wrong?"

Mrs. Brodie looked up, blinking at us as if we were the ones acting strangely. "Oh, darling, I'm fine," she said, her tone as casual as if she'd just asked for a cup of tea. "How do you like my 'get well soon' card for Dr. Henderson? It's actually for his cat, who's been feeling a bit under the weather."

Topher's mouth opened, then closed, as he struggled to process what he was seeing. "Why did you scare me like that? I thought something was seriously wrong!"

She set her crafts aside, her voice softening. "I'm so sorry, I didn't mean to scare you. I just wanted to talk to you about something, that's all."

Topher looked like he was still trying to catch up, but he nodded, stepping closer to the bed. "What is it?"

Mrs. Brodie took a deep breath, her expression softening into something more serious. "I've been thinking a lot about what's best for my recovery, and I've decided that my wish is for you to live with me and to bring your lovely Kathleen to stay with us. You know, for my health."

Topher blinked, his brain clearly short-circuiting. "Wait, what? For your health?"

She gave him a sweet smile. "Yes, dear. The doctor said I need to be near the warmth of family."

Topher sighed loudly. "Fine, I was already thinking of bringing you to my house in the Garden District. It's got everything. Close to the hospital. Quiet. Pool and hot tub. Every comfort that money can buy.

But Mrs. Brodie shook her head firmly. "No, it has to be my house, Topher."

"Mom, I have plenty of room. You'd have your own wing! And there's a pool. You love pools!"

He didn't give her a chance to respond before launching into more reasons. "Plus, the house has a home theater. You could watch your shows on a screen as big as a wall!"

Mrs. Brodie just looked at him with that same calm smile, clearly unmoved by his pitch. "Topher, I appreciate the offer, but I don't need a mansion. I need you and Kathleen with me, in my little house." She paused. "It's for my health."

Topher was stubborn. "Mom. My place has heated floors. Think of it. You hate cold feet. Never again, and you don't even need socks to achieve it. Warm feet, and you can show off your perfect manicure." He grinned. "How can you say no? *And* I have a personal chef! He can make those soufflés you love!"

Mrs. Brodie chuckled softly, patting the bed beside her. "Oh, sweetheart, all the heated floors in the world can't replace the comfort of having the two of you in my own home."

My heart skipped a beat. The three of us? Living together in her house? This was not part of the plan.

But Mrs. Brodie was firm. "Topher, I want to be in my own house, surrounded by my things. It's where I'll feel the most at ease, and where I'll get better. I don't want a chef or a maid. Besides," she added with a mischievous glint in her eye, "it'll give me and Kathleen a chance to get to know each other better."

"But, Mom, who's going to do the cooking and the cleaning?" Topher asked, sounding more like a lost kid than a billionaire with an army of staff.

Without thinking, the words slipped out of my mouth. "We will. Of course, we'll stay with you, Mrs. Brodie."

As soon as I said it, a wave of panic hit me. What was I doing? Agreeing to live under the same roof as Topher? But then I saw the way Mrs. Brodie's face lit up, and somehow, it felt like the right thing to do, even if it meant navigating the awkwardness—and potential disaster—that was sure to come.

Topher shot me an annoyed look. But there wasn't much he could say without looking like the bad guy. Instead, he sighed, rubbing the back of his neck. "If that's what you want, Mom."

Mrs. Brodie beamed, clearly pleased with herself. "It is. Thank you, both of you. And Kathleen, call me Josephine."

As we left the hospital, the weight of what I'd just agreed to started to settle in. I turned to Topher as we reached the parking lot. "Exactly how big is your mom's house?"

Topher hesitated, a slight grimace crossing his face. "Small. Very small."

I frowned. "How small?"

He sighed, clearly dreading this as much as I was. "Small enough that we'll have to share a bedroom."

5

TOPHER HADN'T LIED about how small his mom's house was. It was a classic New Orleans shotgun house, tidy, with just enough space to get by. Cozy, some would call it, if they were trying to be polite.

Despite its size, the place had charm. The walls were covered in eclectic art: bright, bold pieces that gave the space a lively feel. Each room was a burst of color, from the deep blues and greens in the kitchen to the warm yellows and reds in the living room.

Topher, all six feet four inches of him, looked almost comically out of place in the living room, like a giant trying to fit into a dollhouse. He had changed out of his suit but was still dressed for the office, sporting crisp slacks and a button-down shirt that looked far too polished for the task at hand. He was crouched under a table, his broad shoulders nearly wedged into the cramped space as he fiddled with the internet router.

"I just fixed the internet," he announced as he stood, brushing off his hands with the same precision he probably used after closing a big deal. "It was down because Mom plugged an old toaster in next to the router. Completely fried the signal."

I coughed. "Wait, plugged a toaster next to the router?"

"Yeah, I'm guessing that there aren't enough outlets in the kitchen." Topher sighed. "I'll have to explain to her that Wi-Fi doesn't mix well with kitchen appliances, especially ones that have a habit of short-circuiting."

As I looked around the room, my eyes landed on a wall entirely covered with magazine covers. Fortune, Forbes, GQ, Vanity Fair, even some obscure business mags I'd never heard of.

Each one featured a ridiculously good-looking man in a designer suit, striking that classic billionaire pose: chin tilted, smolder dialed to ten, staring off like the meaning of life was hiding just out of frame.

I walked closer. They all looked vaguely familiar. Then it hit me.

They were all Topher. Every. Single. One. Some had him mid-laugh with supermodels. One had him in front of a private jet with "Brodie" emblazoned on the wing in gold lettering.

When I first saw him at the airport—and later at the hospital—I hadn't recognized him at all. He was just another arrogant guy in a suit, someone who got under my skin. But now, seeing these magazine covers, it clicked. This was *the* Topher Brodie, the hometown boy who somehow made a gazillion dollars doing... well, something with money. I wasn't entirely sure what, but apparently, he was good enough at it to end up on the cover of every financial magazine known to man. The pieces were finally falling into place, and I couldn't help but wonder how I hadn't connected the dots sooner.

I cleared my throat. "So, what exactly does your company do?"

Topher's eyes lit up, clearly thrilled to elaborate. "We strategically hedge against potential market volatilities through a complex series of predictive algorithms. Then, we leverage these insights to invest at exponentially higher interest rates. We acquire undervalued debt portfolios, which we then dynamically reposition within the market using a proprietary blend of quantitative easing and fiscal alchemy. Pretty fascinating, don't you think?"

I squinted. "I'll take your word for it." Crossing my arms, I glanced at the magazine covers again. "Didn't know I was dealing with the world's most eligible bachelor. Should I be asking for your autograph?"

He shot me an annoyed look. "My PR team's in charge of those. I'd never even talked with half of those women before the shoots."

"Right," I said, still trying to wrap my head around being in a fake relationship with a billionaire.

He cleared his throat, and when he spoke, he sounded a bit weary. "It's all part of the image I'm selling. Looking the part is half the job."

I glanced back at the wall of magazine covers, and a wave of unease washed over me. Here was this guy, looking like he'd just stepped out of a fashion shoot. And then there was me. I was definitely not a supermodel, and not a high-powered businesswoman by anyone's definition. My resume was a patchwork of jobs I hadn't even managed to hold onto. I couldn't help but feel a pang of inadequacy.

Who was going to believe that *I* was dating *him*? The math wasn't mathing. It was like adding two plus two and ending up with a potato. How in the world was I going to pull this off?

The reality of the situation was settling in. "Where are we supposed to sleep?" Staying here with him in such close quarters... kind of made me want to throw up.

Topher walked to the only closed door in the house. "This is my childhood bedroom," he said, giving the handle a tentative jiggle. The door didn't budge. He frowned, applying more force.

With one final push, the door popped open with a loud creak. Before we could even take a step inside, a cascade of holiday decorations burst out like an overstuffed closet finally giving way. A string of tangled Christmas lights flew at us, wrapping around my arm like some sort of festive snake, while a deflated Santa hat drifted lazily to the floor.

"Oh, well, hello," I murmured, trying to untangle myself from the lights as a plastic Easter egg rolled out and bounced off my shoe.

Topher stood there, wide-eyed, as a few more holiday items tumbled out, including a glittery Valentine's Day heart smacked him right in the chest, and a Halloween witch on a broomstick landed at his feet with a cackle that echoed through the tiny hallway.

As we stepped into the bedroom, I immediately felt a chill run down my spine. The room was an explosion of every holiday imaginable. Christmas lights tangled with Halloween cobwebs, Easter eggs mixed in with Thanksgiving cornucopias, and a giant inflatable turkey wearing a Santa hat wedged in the corner. But what caught my eye, and made my stomach drop, was the massive, grinning clown face that loomed from the corner, illuminated by a flickering, ghostly light.

"Oh, heck no," I whispered, taking an involuntary step back.

Topher, oblivious, wandered farther into the room, casually brushing aside a Halloween bat that had swooped down from a string of Christmas lights.

"What's wrong?" he asked, glancing over his shoulder at me.

"That." I pointed a shaky finger at the clown. "That thing. Why is it looking at me like that?"

Topher turned to the clown, a giant inflatable with a face painted in garish colors, its eyes wide and unblinking. A creepy smile stretched from ear to ear, and I could swear its head tilted slightly in my direction.

"It's just a Halloween decoration," he said, barely suppressing a grin. "You're not seriously scared of that, are you?"

"Of course not," I retorted, but my voice edged toward panic, betraying me.

Topher chuckled and walked over to the clown, giving it a nudge. It swayed ominously, its creepy grin never faltering. "It's just an inflatable, Kathleen. Look, I'll even deflate it for you." He leaned down to find the valve, but just as he did, the clown's mechanical arm sprang to life, raising a butcher knife in a slow, menacing motion.

"It's armed!" I screamed, stumbling back into a pile of faux gravestones and knocking over a menorah that was somehow nestled in a bed of plastic shamrocks.

Topher burst out laughing, nearly doubling over as he watched me try to scramble away from the murderous clown. "It's not armed, it's automated! It's supposed to do that!"

"That's not helping!" I frantically waved my arms to ward off the imaginary attack. The clown's knife-wielding hand continued its mechanical swing, and my heart pounded in my chest.

Topher, still shaking with laughter, reached over and pulled the plug on the inflatable. It hissed as it began to deflate, the knife-wielding arm sagging pathetically as the clown crumpled to the floor, landing on top of a stack of Fourth of July sparklers.

"There, see? Harmless," he said, grinning as he turned back to me.

"Harmless?" I echoed, still trying to catch my breath. "That thing was one creepy laugh away from giving me a heart attack!"

Topher wiped a tear from his eye, clearly amused by the whole ordeal. "You're seriously afraid of a deflating clown?"

"Clowns are bad enough," I crossed my arms defensively. "But clowns with weapons? That's a hard no."

Topher's face relaxed into a big grin. "I didn't expect to laugh today, so thank you for that."

"You're welcome, I guess." I rolled my eyes. "I take it this isn't how your room looked when you were a kid?"

Topher shot me a dry look. "Oh, sure. Every teenage boy dreams of waking up to an inflatable Santa and a bunch of heart-shaped glitter bombs. I guess I've been gone so long that my mom decided to use my room for storage."

He grimaced and nudged a stack of shamrock-covered St. Patrick's Day hats that were somehow tangled in a mess of Fourth of July sparklers. "And here I thought my worst nightmare was getting roped into a reality dating show."

I glanced around at the chaos. "At this rate, we'll be lucky if we can even find the bed under all this."

We both turned to face the bed. Or what I assumed was the bed, given that it was buried under a mountain of patriotic decorations. American flags, Uncle Sam hats, and red, white, and blue streamers were piled so high that they nearly obscured a cardboard cutout of George Washington, who somehow managed to remain upright in the chaos. His stern expression seemed to judge us for even thinking we could sleep in such a place.

Topher sighed, rubbing his temples. "All right. We need a plan. You start untangling whatever holiday monstrosity is hanging from the ceiling, and I'll try to find the actual bed under George Washington and his army of flags."

It soon became clear that the best way to tackle the chaos was to organize everything into boxes, one for each holiday. For about five minutes, we worked in silence, the only sounds being the rustle of tinsel and the occasional squeak from a rogue rubber bat.

After shoving a gang of Thanksgiving turkeys into a box, Topher straightened up, wiping dust off his hands like he'd just finished a major corporate deal. "You know, you're probably way better at organizing this stuff than I am. Plus, I've got some work to catch up on. Maybe you should take charge here. I need to head over to my place in the Garden District. It's got a better setup for work."

I shot him a look that could have melted the Santa still half-inflated in the corner. My hands were full of tangled Christmas lights, and I could feel the frustration bubbling up. Of course, Captain Corporate would decide that this wasn't the best use of his precious time. Heaven forbid he waste a minute not buried in his work.

"No way are you leaving me alone in here!" I snapped, glaring at him as he glanced longingly at his phone. "Those inflatables might decide to stage another attack, and I'm not about to face them solo."

Inwardly, I fumed. Topher was already plotting his escape to his mansion. *Must be nice to have a 'better setup.'* He probably thought he could just delegate everything to me and swoop back in when it was all neatly sorted and boxed up. But there was no way I was letting him off that easily.

Topher let out a small, annoyed sigh but quickly gave in, his shoulders slumping a bit. "Fine," he muttered. "Guess my work can wait. But so that you know, I'll probably need to spend most nights at my mansion until my mom gets out of the hospital. The setup there helps me stay on top of things."

Good, I thought, resisting the urge to fist-pump. If he camped out at his mansion every night, I wouldn't have to worry about sharing a room with him. His unhealthy obsession with work was finally doing something worthwhile. For me, at least.

Before long, we made enough progress to reveal what the room must have looked like when Topher was a kid.

Posters of the periodic table and math equations adorned the walls, along with gleaming medals and scores of trophies. I could almost picture a younger Topher, lost in his world of numbers and science. A stack of books screamed "child prodigy," with titles like "Advanced Calculus for Beginners" and "Quantum Physics Made Simple."

"Wow," I said. "I didn't realize I'd stumbled into the headquarters of a future Nobel Prize winner."

Topher glanced around. "Yeah, well, I guess I was a bit of a nerd."

I pointed to a model of the solar system hanging from the ceiling. "You've got the entire universe up there, literally."

"I was really into astronomy for a while. Thought I might be an astronaut until I realized I couldn't handle the idea of being stuck in a small capsule with other people for months."

"So, instead of exploring the stars, you decided to conquer Wall Street?"

He shrugged. "Something like that. But I am looking into buying a spaceship."

I stared at him, half expecting him to be joking, but the look on his face was completely serious. "Wait, you're actually trying to buy a spaceship?"

"Yep. Space tourism is going to be the next big thing."

Right. The sheer disparity between our lives would be laughable if it weren't so unsettling. There he was, casually discussing the purchase of a spaceship while I was skimping on groceries to keep the lights on.

Before I could dwell too long on the absurdity of it all, Topher said, "I think we've got the room in good enough shape. Let's move these boxes out so you can bring your stuff in here."

I blinked, shaking off the lingering haze of disbelief, and nodded. "Yeah, let's do that."

I started unpacking my things. It didn't take long. There wasn't much to begin with. A couple of small suitcases filled with clothes and mementos, a handful of books, and a small box of papers I'd been avoiding.

"This is all you brought?" Topher sounded astonished.

"Yeah, well, I'm a woman of simple tastes." I tried to sound breezy, even though the reality was far from simple.

His eyes lingered on the box of papers, and before I could stop him, he reached out. "Here, let me—"

"Don't touch those!" The words flew out of my mouth like a reflex.

He jerked back, startled, sending a few papers fluttering to the floor. "I'm sorry. I didn't mean to—"

"It's fine," I snapped, quickly gathering the papers and shoving them back into the bottom of my suitcase. My hands were shaking, and I hoped he didn't notice. "I just... haven't had time to deal with them yet. I need to go through them at some point."

The truth was, I wasn't sure I'd ever be ready to go through those papers. Every time I even thought about sorting them, I felt that sinking feeling in my gut, like I was about to uncover something else about my parents that would disappoint me even more than I already was.

But I didn't have time to dwell on that right now. We had bigger fish to fry. Or, more accurately, a house to transform. Mrs. Brodie was going to be discharged soon, and this place needed to be more of a "recovery haven" and less of a "quaint disaster zone."

That meant Topher and I would have to, heaven help us, work together.

I cleared my throat. "You know, if we're going to pull this off, we need to get to know each other better. There's no way your mom will believe we've been dating for six months if we can't even answer basic questions about each other."

He looked up from the box he was sorting, clearly not thrilled with the idea. "Okay, fine," he said with a sigh, "ask me a question."

"Do you have any brothers or sisters?"

"Nope, only child."

"Same here." *Great, two only children. We're probably both used to getting our own way. This should be interesting.* "What do you do for fun?"

"I like to go all out on my rowing machine, pushing myself to the limit until my muscles burn."

Even his idea of fun sounded like torture. "And here I thought fun was supposed to be, you know, fun."

He straightened up, his tone defensive. "It is fun. There's a real rush in pushing your body to the limit and breaking your personal records." He eyed me, challenging. "So, what do you consider fun?"

I tried to ease the tension. "Well, think less actual marathon, more movie marathon. Where did you go to college?"

"Brown. You?"

Brown, huh? I could picture him and his crew team buddies rowing down the river, discussing their self-designed majors and shouting quotes from Diderot and Foucault at each other between strokes. They probably organized protests for environmental justice in between putting on an experimental theater production and debating existentialism, the ethics of modern economics, and whether 'Inception' really deserves its cult status.

"I went to Duke for a while, but didn't finish. What's your favorite food?"

"I have a chef who handles all my meals to make sure I get balanced macros, vitamins, the whole thing. Though sometimes I'm just too busy to eat."

Too busy to eat? What kind of person gets too busy to eat? "You said you haven't visited your mom in a while. Why not?"

His whole demeanor shifted, and he stiffened like I'd hit a nerve. "Next question."

Clearly a touchy subject. "Okay, fine, what's it like being a billionaire?"

Topher leaned against the doorway. "Honestly? If I acted like a billionaire, I wouldn't be one. Every penny spent is a penny that could've earned more pennies. There's no room for indulgence if you want to stay on top."

"You do have a private jet, though, right?"

"Of course, time is money. Why waste it waiting around for commercial flights at airports?"

"And how many houses do you own? I mean, I know about the one here in the Garden District, but you spend most of your time in New York, right?"

"Well, there are a few more than just my house in New Orleans and my penthouse in Manhattan, but each property I own is a solid investment. Take my castle in England: it's appreciated three-hundred percent since I bought it. And my yacht has risen four-hundred percent in value."

I nearly choked on my drink. "So, just the one yacht, or are we talking a fleet?"

"Just the one. A single yacht is more than enough for personal relaxation and hosting important business meetings."

Just the one. As if one yacht is perfectly normal. He really did live in a different world. "You know, I sometimes fantasize about what I'd do if I won the lottery. I'd give a lot of it away, and help out people who need it."

Topher scoffed, his tone edged with disdain. "Lottery tickets are a fool's investment. People who buy them might as well be burning their money."

I bristled slightly, defending my daydream. "It's just a bit of fun, not a financial strategy. Besides, dreaming big doesn't cost anything. You have so much... Do you give to any charities?"

He hesitated, and his jaw tightened slightly. "Look, I believe in investments, not handouts. It's better to invest in something that can grow and create more opportunities. Handouts don't solve the root problems; they just create dependency."

His words hit me harder than I expected. *So, not only is he a workaholic, but he doesn't even believe in helping people who are struggling.* A knot formed in my stomach. *This is who I'm supposed to pretend I'm in love with?*

I forced a smile. "Interesting perspective. You're all about the bottom line, huh?"

"Someone has to be," he replied, as if that was the most obvious thing in the world.

"Well, I believe that life's about more than just work and money." I tried to keep my tone light but firm. "Like taking a day off just because you feel like it or giving away something to make someone else's day better."

Topher's expression shifted to one of disbelief. "You don't see the value in working hard, do you?"

I narrowed my eyes. "And you don't see the value in slowing down every once in a while, do you?"

He gave me a pointed look. "I don't get people who don't take work seriously."

"And I don't get people who can't switch off."

We stared at each other for a moment, the tension thickening between us. It was like we were from entirely different worlds, each struggling to understand how the other could live the way they did.

This was going to be four long weeks.

6

I STRETCHED out on the couch in Topher's mom's house, quiet all around me. No voices, no footsteps, not even the faint sound of someone breathing nearby. I was utterly alone.

And where was Topher? Oh, right—at his mansion. After we cleaned the bedroom, Topher bolted, saying he had work to do. Later, he texted that he'd be spending the night at his place. Cool, no big deal. Just left me here to fend for myself in a house I barely knew.

So, yep. I spent the whole night alone in a strange house.

And it was *glorious*.

No one telling me I should be working harder. No smug looks from across the room. No lectures about how I'm "wasting my potential" because I wasn't "squeezing every last drop of productivity out of the day." Yes, those were his exact words. It was just me, that ridiculously comfy couch, one of Mrs. Brodie's dog-eared bestsellers, and the sweet, sweet absence of Topher hovering nearby, silently judging me for not treating work like it's the meaning of life.

Topher's mom had surgery before dawn. The plan was for him to visit her once she was out of recovery later that afternoon. I'd texted him that morning, asking how the surgery went. He said everything went well, and she would likely need a few days of recovery. Which meant...

I had a few days all to myself.

I could read, I could nap, I could do absolutely nothing. Sure, I needed to figure out what my next job would be, but the idea of spending a few days like this? It felt like a surprise vacation. Topher might pop in now and then to check on things, but with his mom in the hospital and work dragging him back to his mansion, I didn't expect him to stick around much. And honestly? That was fine by me.

I could practically hear the quiet stretching out ahead of me, endless and peaceful.

Then, like a marching band crashing a silent retreat, the tranquility was shattered.

I heard the unmistakable sound of a key turning in the lock. Before I could even react, the front door swung open, and in bustled a short, round woman with tight gray curls, dressed in a floral blouse so bright it could be seen from space. She carried a basket of muffins as if it were her ticket to wherever she wanted to go. Without so much as a glance in my direction, she let herself in and closed the door behind her.

"Yoo-hoo! Anybody home?" she called out, loud enough to wake the dead, her eyes already scanning the room as if she owned the place.

I shot up from the couch, bewildered. "Uh, hi?"

"Oh, you must be Kathleen!" The woman breezed right in, beaming at me like we were old friends. "Josephine told me all about you. I'm Gladys from next door, and I've been keeping an eye on the place while she's in the hospital. You know, just making sure things are running smoothly. I've got a key in case of emergencies." She winked as if that explained why she was making herself at home, already plopping down in the armchair across from the couch, setting her muffin basket on the coffee table.

"That's... uh... nice of you." I was trying to process the fact that a stranger had just let herself into the house.

"Oh, honey, Josephine called and told me about her son finally bringing home a girlfriend. It's all very exciting!" She winked again, like we were sharing some secret joke. "So, where is he?"

"Uh, Topher's working." I tried to sound casual. "He had some things to take care of."

Gladys leaned forward, narrowing her eyes. "Didn't seem like he spent the night here, though. I saw him leave yesterday afternoon, and I never saw him return. Where is he now?"

I could feel her nosy gaze burning into me and coughed. "He's, um, at his place in the Garden District, but he'll be back soon."

"Oh, *will* he now?" One eyebrow shot up as she leaned in closer. "Seems a little odd, doesn't it? To leave his girlfriend all alone here on your first night together?"

My stomach twisted. It was clear we were being snooped on, and if this nosy neighbor figured out we weren't really dating, it would only be a matter of time before it got back to Topher's mom. The last thing I needed was for her to know this whole relationship was a sham. And then what? I'd be homeless. Again. I had no job, no place to stay, and the one thing keeping me off the streets was this ridiculous fake relationship.

I whipped out my phone, my heart pounding in my chest, and shot off a text to Topher: *Get over here right now. Your neighbor, Gladys, is asking too many questions. I think she's on to us.*

I glanced at Gladys, who was still staring at me like I was a puzzle she was determined to solve. She cleared her throat. "So, how long have you two been together? Josephine didn't give me many details."

I forced a smile. "We haven't been together too long."

"Well, you two must be *very* serious if you're already staying here while Josephine's in the hospital. Isn't that something?" She eyed me with a twinkle that could only mean one thing—gossip. "So, when are you moving in together for good?"

I nearly choked. Luckily, my phone buzzed with Topher's text: *On my way. Don't let her find out the truth.*

Great. No pressure.

Trying to keep my cool, I smiled again. "We're taking things slow. No rush to move in together or anything." My voice cracked slightly.

Gladys gave me a look that said she didn't believe me, but before she could dig deeper, her face shifted into one of those concerned, motherly looks. "By the way, how are Topher's headaches? Josephine's been so worried about them lately."

My stomach flipped. *Headaches?* What was I supposed to say? "He's feeling better every day." Hopefully, I didn't sound completely clueless.

Gladys tilted her head, one eyebrow creeping upward in skepticism. "Hmm, well, that's good to hear." She leaned in, lowering her voice like she was about to reveal the juiciest gossip of the century. "You know, Topher was a *real* math nerd when he was in high school. I'm talking calculators in his pockets and spreadsheets for fun. I mean, no offense, but I didn't think he had it in him to snag someone like *you*." She paused, giving me another dramatic once-over. "Honestly, I was starting to think I'd never see a girl walk through this door unless she was getting tutored."

I let out an awkward laugh, trying to deflect. "Well, I guess people can surprise you..."

"Oh, *you* sure did." Gladys wagged her finger like she'd solved a mystery. "I'm telling you, no one ever thought Topher would bring a woman home. And here you are, staying in his mom's house. So, what's the story? How'd you two meet?"

"Oh, you know, we just... bumped into each other." I tried to sound casual while my brain scrambled for a distraction. "So, um, how long have you lived next door?"

Gladys stared for a beat too long, but she went along with the subject change. "Oh, long enough to know Topher's never been the relationship type. Until you, that is. I'm guessing a proposal's coming soon, huh?"

I nearly choked on air. *Proposal?* We weren't even a real couple!

I let out a nervous laugh, trying to maintain my composure. "Uh, we're not there yet. We're just, you know, still in the getting-to-know-each-other phase."

Gladys's mouth twitched, somewhere between amusement and disbelief. "Honey, I've lived here long enough to know when something's serious. And trust me, it's *serious*. You'll be picking out wedding venues before you know it. I can already see you in white!"

Just as I was about to die of nervous laughter, the front door swung open, and in strolled Topher, looking slightly out of breath. "Gladys, always a pleasure," he said, pulling her into a quick, polite hug. "But no time to chat. Busy day, you know how it is."

Gladys didn't miss a beat, eyes sparkling with curiosity. "Oh, I'm sure it's busy with all the *romance* in the air." She gave me a knowing look that made my stomach tighten.

Topher barely blinked. "Right, busy with that and, you know, work. But we've got to run because we're heading to visit my mom at the hospital."

Gladys's face lit up. "So, when did you two first realize it was love?"

Topher plastered on a tight smile and completely ignored her question. "It's been great to see you. Thanks so much for the muffins, Gladys."

He reached for the container, clearly hoping to do a clean handoff and escort her to the door in one graceful maneuver.

But Gladys was faster.

"Oh, I'll just pop them in the kitchen for you," she chirped, side-stepping him like she'd been dodging slick moves since before he was born.

Before either of us could protest, she was off to the kitchen. Topher turned to me, eyes narrow. "Why did you let her in?"

I glared right back. "She had a *key*, Topher! What was I supposed to do, tackle her?"

He threw his hands up in silent exasperation. "I leave you alone for a few hours, and suddenly, my mom's nosy neighbor has moved in."

I snorted. "Oh, like you've been the model host. Where were you? Oh, right, at your *mansion*."

His eyes flicked to the kitchen. "She said she was just going to drop off the muffins, but she's been in there for a while... What is she *doing*?"

We both craned our necks to listen, but all we could hear were faint clinks and rustling. I raised an eyebrow at Topher. "You think she's rearranging the silverware? Because it sounds like she's rearranging the silverware."

A thud followed the series of clinks. Gladys's voice floated out cheerfully, "Oopsie!"

Topher pinched the bridge of his nose. "You were the one who let her in."

"For the millionth time, she had a *key*. I didn't let her in. She *materialized*."

Finally, after what felt like an eternity, Gladys reemerged from the kitchen, looking pleased with herself. "All set! You two enjoy those muffins now." She winked.

Topher crossed his arms. "What was that thud we heard?"

"Oh, that?" Gladys waved her hand dismissively. "I was just searching through your mother's cabinets for some Saran Wrap to cover the muffins. It's like a scavenger hunt in there—stuff crammed everywhere! I found the Saran Wrap all the way in the back, behind what appeared to be a jar of expired pickles. I had to pull out half your mom's Tupperware to get to it. That was the thud. But don't worry, I reorganized a little! *Anywhoodle*, muffins are safe now, wrapped tight. You're welcome!"

With a satisfied nod, she headed for the door, but not before throwing one last look over her shoulder. "I'll be watching—er, *checking in*—on you two!"

As soon as the door clicked shut, I let out a long, exhausted breath. "Well, that was a disaster."

Topher ran a hand through his hair like he was about to pull it out. "You think? She's going to be watching every move we make." He grabbed his laptop. "Let me do a little work before we go visit my mom." He typed for a moment, but then froze mid-motion and groaned like the world was ending. "The internet's slowing down again." He whirled around, narrowing his eyes at me like I was the Wi-Fi saboteur. "Did you do something to it?"

I blinked, incredulous. "Me? I didn't do anything! I haven't even been on the internet!"

I couldn't believe this guy. He could run a multi-million dollar company, but he couldn't survive *five minutes* with slow Wi-Fi. It was like watching a grown man unravel because his lifeline to endless work emails had been cut. What kind of person is so obsessed with working that a minor internet outage sends them into a tailspin? *Unbelievable.*

Topher paced, running a hand through his hair again. "I can't work like this. I'll figure it out later." He glanced toward the window, his eyes narrowing like Gladys might already be out there plotting. "Let's just go see my mom." He looked down at his crisp slacks and button-up. "Let me change my clothes first."

I nodded absently. "I'm going to have one of those muffins." All the stress was making me hungry. In the kitchen, I froze. *Wait a minute.* The muffins weren't wrapped. Gladys had made such a big deal about the Saran Wrap, and yet there they were, muffin tops exposed to the world like nothing had happened. *Weird.*

I glanced down the hall to tell Topher about the muffins, but when I saw him, every word I ever knew flew right out of my head. *Muffins? What muffins?* There was only Topher's muscular back as he pulled off his shirt, the bedroom door slightly ajar.

And, wow.

He was... *in good shape.* Not just "Oh, he works out occasionally," in good shape. *Really good shape.* His back was all lean muscle, flexing with every movement as he tugged his shirt off. I blinked, my brain doing a weird thing where it completely short-circuited. Was this the same guy who spent his life obsessing over work? This was not the image I had in my head of him. At all.

I should've turned away, should've said something, *anything,* but instead, I just stood there, staring. He moved fluidly, obviously not aware of the effect he was having, as he grabbed a Henley and slipped it over his head. His muscles rippled with every movement. The shirt clung to him as he adjusted it, and my eyes lingered far longer than I'd care to admit.

I thought back to everything Gladys had said about him being a math nerd. If this was what math did to a person, maybe I should've paid more attention in algebra.

7

WE DIDN'T EVEN MAKE it to the curb before the bickering started.

By the time we slid into Topher's waiting car, we were already mid-argument. That's right—Topher had a driver. And this was not the limo driver with the walker from the airport, mind you. This one looked like his only job was to wait around until Topher snapped his fingers and demanded to be whisked somewhere *important*. Like the hospital. Where we were headed. To visit his recovering mother.

With zero flowers.

I shot Topher a glare as we marched toward the hospital entrance. "Flowers are not frivolous!"

"For the last time, Mom doesn't want flowers. I mean, she doesn't need anything, but if we get her something, she'd rather have something useful."

"Useful?" I threw up my hands. "Oh, sure, let's grab her a screwdriver set. Maybe a nice set of pliers to really brighten her day!"

"She doesn't need something that's just going to die in a week." His eyes were glued to his phone, which only made me more irritated. There we were, visiting his mom in the hospital, and the guy couldn't even pull his face away from his work for five minutes.

"Yeah, well, she doesn't need you glued to your phone either, but here we are," I shot back. "Are you seriously working right now?"

He didn't even bother looking up. "I'm not working. I'm just checking in."

"*Just checking in*?" I stopped dead in my tracks, letting out a frustrated huff. "Topher, we're here to visit your mom, not to make sure your company's stocks haven't crashed in the last five minutes."

Miraculously, he slipped the phone into his pocket. We marched toward the hospital entrance in stiff, irritated silence. The tension clung to the air between us like static. But the moment we stepped inside, the sterile smell of the hospital hit me. It was a scent that always brought back memories. Bad memories.

Topher's pace slowed as we approached the recovery wing, and worry creased his forehead.

At his mom's door, a nurse stepped out, smiling warmly. "You can go in. She's doing well. The surgery went smoothly."

His mom was lying in bed, looking pale but peaceful, her eyes closed. Her hair was a little disheveled, and the lines on her face showed exhaustion, but when she opened her eyes and saw us, her whole face lit up.

"Hey, you two," she said weakly, her voice full of warmth.

Topher walked over to her bedside and gently adjusted her pillow, smoothing it with careful hands. "Hey, Mom."

"There's my boy." She reached up and patted his arm. Then her gaze shifted to me, and despite her exhaustion, she smiled. "And Kathleen, sweetie, thank you for coming."

Topher moved closer, sitting down on the edge of her bed. Without missing a beat, he stroked her hair back gently, as if it were something he'd done a thousand times. "How are you feeling?" He spoke softly.

His mom squeezed his hand weakly. "Tired, but okay. The doctor said everything went well."

Topher nodded, his thumb absentmindedly brushing over the back of her hand in circles. "I'm glad, Mom. You had us worried."

She smiled again, her eyes flicking to me with warmth. "I'm just glad I woke up to see two of my favorite people. I feel better already with you both here."

I returned her smile, but inside, I was still processing how tender this whole moment felt.

As much as Topher could be the most infuriating person on the planet, seeing him being this gentle and loving toward his mom made me see him differently. There was a sweetness to him I hadn't expected. Underneath all the bickering, the workaholic tendencies, the constant tension between us, he was kind. At least to his mom.

She shifted and squeezed Topher's hand. "I've been thinking about taking a break from Muses."

Topher leaned in. "You've been talking about this for a while. Are you ready?"

She nodded. "The doctors say I need to slow down. I've got a good team in place, but it's hard to let go. Muses has been my life for the past decade, but it's time."

Topher's concern was apparent. "If you need anything, let me know."

She smiled, her eyes twinkling. "Maybe it'll give me more time to meddle in your life."

Just as I was starting to wrap my head around this whole new version of Topher, the door creaked open and a tall man in a white coat walked in. Dr. Julius was the kind of doctor who looked like he belonged in an old-school medical TV drama. He had salt-and-pepper hair, thick glasses perched on his nose, and a clipboard tucked under his arm. His calm, authoritative presence somehow made you feel both safe and as though you were about to be scolded for not eating enough vegetables.

The doctor stepped forward to review her charts and vitals, approaching her bedside. Topher instinctively stepped away from his mom's side and came to stand next to me.

"Ah, good to see you two," Dr. Julius said with a nod, looking at Topher and me. "Your mother's doing remarkably well. In fact, if things continue like this, I don't see why she can't go home tomorrow."

Topher's mom beamed. "Home tomorrow? That's wonderful!"

Dr. Julius smiled. "Yes, she's recovering even faster than expected. We'll run a few more tests in the morning, but barring any surprises, you'll be out of here by tomorrow afternoon." He smiled at her and gave another quick nod.

It was right at that moment—totally out of nowhere—that Topher reached over and grabbed my hand.

It felt awkward at first, like some forced performance for his mother's benefit. His grip was a little stiff, his fingers slightly tense. But then something shifted. As Dr. Julius continued talking about the final tests, Topher's grip loosened, his fingers relaxing in mine. And it didn't feel so forced anymore. His hand was warm, solid, and... nice. Really nice, actually.

I tried to keep my expression neutral, pretending like I wasn't hyper-aware of the fact that Topher, Mr. Annoying Workaholic Extraordinaire, was holding my hand in this soft, almost reassuring way.

I could feel a slight tingle up my arm, and as awkward as it had started, I found myself not wanting to pull away.

The moment Dr. Julius was gone, Josephine turned to us with a cheery smile. "Oh, I almost forgot to tell you two, I'm not sure if you noticed, but I'm storing some holiday decorations in your old bedroom, Topher."

Topher and I froze. *Some holiday decorations?* That was the understatement of the century. More like, *all the holiday decorations, plus a partridge in a pear tree.* For heaven's sake, you couldn't even see the bed, let alone sleep in it.

"Oh, and don't touch anything," his mother said. "I know exactly where everything is. I have it all just the way I like it."

I shot a quick, wide-eyed glance at Topher, who looked just as horrified as I felt. *Just the way she likes it?* If we hadn't moved half that mess, we'd need to sleep standing up.

Josephine seemed oblivious to the fact that the room had been a hazard zone. "I need to know where everything is for the holidays."

My face must've mirrored Topher's as we stared at his mom, who was looking so peaceful in her hospital bed. She had no idea that Topher's gardener had already hauled most of the stuff into the garage. And I wasn't about to be the one to break it to her.

Suddenly, Topher squeezed my hand. Something shifted in my heart, and I felt for the first time like we were in this together. It didn't feel bad.

Topher shifted uncomfortably, his mouth opening and closing like he was searching for the right thing to say. Finally, he settled on a very noncommittal, "Uh, sure, Mom. We'll figure it out."

The door swung open again, and a nurse bustled in. "Time to let your mom get some rest."

We walked over to his mom's bedside. Without missing a beat, Topher leaned down and kissed her on the forehead, and I followed suit, giving her a gentle kiss on the cheek.

"Get some rest, Mom," Topher said softly, his voice full of warmth.

As we straightened up, I noticed that our hands were still loosely linked. But as we pulled back, our fingers slipped apart. It was strange, the absence of his touch.

The drive back to the house was quiet. There was no bickering, no snarky remarks. By the time we got inside, the night had settled into calm silence, the kind that makes you want to curl up and drift off.

Topher tossed his keys on the counter, turning to me. "I've got a lot of work to catch up on. I'll take the couch tonight," he said, running a hand through his hair. "You take the bedroom."

We moved around the house, checking all the deadbolts and making sure the curtains were drawn tight. The last thing we needed was for Gladys, the nosiest neighbor on the planet, to spot anything suspicious. With all that done, Topher settled onto the couch, and I headed for the bedroom.

I slipped under the covers. With his mom coming home tomorrow, we'd be stuck in her guest room together, pretending to be a happy couple. *Sleeping in the same room.*

8

THE NEXT MORNING started exactly how you'd expect when you're forced to live in a tiny house with a billionaire: with a stranger flown in from New York to fix the Wi-Fi.

I stood there, rubbing my eyes, clutching my coffee like it was the only thing keeping me sane. I watched as the tech guy—who looked like he should be in a corporate boardroom, not crouched under a router in Topher's mom's tiny house—poked around like he was performing brain surgery. All because Topher had declared the Wi-Fi situation "unacceptable."

Topher paced behind him, arms crossed. "It's unstable. I can't run encrypted calls or high-bandwidth data transfers on a connection that drops to hamster-wheel speeds whenever someone microwaves oatmeal."

The tech nodded gravely, as if this were a universally accepted tragedy.

According to Topher, the home network was "nonviable for confidential work."

According to Josephine, he needed to go outside and touch grass.

According to me, I needed stronger coffee.

Meanwhile, Topher was perched at his elaborate computer workstation, surrounded by four monitors, each one displaying some graph or market trend. It was like the command center for a space mission. Only it was tucked into his mom's cramped living room.

"I don't know why you didn't just call the local internet company," I finally said, my patience wearing thin.

He didn't even glance my way. "They don't understand the complexity of my system. This guy built the network for my offices."

I sighed, taking another sip of coffee, already beyond done with this day. But, naturally, it didn't stop there.

Next came Topher's personal chef. Heaven forbid Topher would be required to make his own breakfast. And it wasn't just any breakfast. Oh no. It had to be some gluten-free, dairy-free, fun-free concoction that required more ingredients than a five-course dinner. The chef took over the tiny kitchen, and I had to duck around him to refill my coffee.

And then there was the personal trainer. Yep, Topher had him bring along a rowing machine. I watched, dumbfounded, as the trainer awkwardly tried to wedge the thing through the front door.

As soon as the rowing machine was in place in the already-cramped living room, Topher jumped aboard. He rowed like a man possessed, while barking questions at his technology guy about backup routers and why his *state-of-the-art* Wi-Fi system had dared to fail him. The trainer, standing there like a statue of calm, adjusted Topher's form, as if this were normal behavior.

As if that wasn't enough, Topher's gardener was carrying boxes of holiday decorations back *into* the house. The very same boxes he'd spent hours clearing out of the guest bedroom. The poor gardener was stacking them along the bedroom walls, all perfectly labeled and organized. At the same time, I mentally calculated how many feet of space we'd have left to sleep in. Spoiler alert: not many.

If I stayed in that house a second longer, surrounded by Topher's tech crisis and workout obsession, I was going to snap.

"I'm going for a walk," I announced, though I didn't think anyone was listening.

The second I stepped outside, however, I regretted it. There, standing right on the front lawn like she'd been waiting for me, stood Ms. Nosy herself, Gladys, in all her floral tracksuit glory.

"Well, well, if it isn't the early bird!" Gladys chirped, her eyes twinkling with nosiness. She winked as if we were both in on some shared secret. "Out for a stroll?"

I plastered on a smile. "Just needed some air."

"Oh, I don't blame you, sweetie." Gladys nodded like she had cracked the code. "Oh, and by the way, I noticed your curtains were drawn last night. *Smart move.* You never know who's watching. Some people around here have no respect for privacy."

I blinked, trying not to laugh or cry. "Right, well, I should keep walking."

"Good idea, dear!" she called after me, probably already plotting her next surveillance operation. "Get those steps in!"

As I walked farther down the street, the weight of the morning slowly began to lift off my shoulders. I could hear birds chirping, the distant hum of a lawnmower, and the soft rustle of leaves in the breeze. Breathing in the calm, I let myself finally relax.

I wandered down different streets, letting the sun warm my face as the stress slowly unwound from my body. It felt better than I'd expected. By the time I finally looped around back to the house, I was ready to face the madness again.

But when I stepped inside, I was met with a familiar and exasperating sight: Topher, freshly showered, dressed in a sharp suit, sitting at his elaborate computer setup. The room was still buzzing with energy from the flurry of people coming and going, the equipment being moved, and conversations happening in low tones. But Topher's focus was entirely on his screens, his eyes darting between charts, emails, and whatever else his empire demanded. He wasn't furiously rowing this time. No, he'd upgraded to furiously working.

He glanced up as I walked in. "Enjoy your little escape?"

"Immensely. Gladys says hi, by the way. She wants to know if you've considered getting a rowing machine that doesn't take up half the living room."

"Oh, Gladys wonders about that?" His tone was completely deadpan.

"She also thinks you need to stop stressing and relax."

Topher paused for a second before shaking his head. "I don't need advice on life balance from Gladys, thank you very much."

"Work, work, work," I muttered, shaking my head. "You'd think your company would implode if you took an hour off. I mean, that's Gladys talking."

He smirked but didn't look up from the screens. "Kathleen, you may not understand the concept of 'work,' but some of us know that taking time off can cost you opportunities."

His words hit a sore spot, but I refused to show it. "You know, Topher, some of us know that all that 'never stopping' can cost you the things that matter."

He hesitated for a moment, his fingers pausing on the keyboard. Then he nodded. "I'd rather be overworked than have regrets."

I swallowed hard. "Trust me, I know all about regrets. And sometimes, no matter how hard you work, you can't get back what you've lost."

Topher's expression shifted. For once, he didn't have a sharp reply or a quick comeback. Instead, he lifted his eyes, and there was something almost gentle in the way he looked at me. It was as if, in that moment, he was seeing me differently, realizing there was more to me than he'd first assumed.

But before he could speak, the front door creaked open. In walked Josephine, much earlier than expected, escorted by a nurse.

"Mom!" Topher jumped up from his fancy ergonomic chair the moment he saw her. His voice was warm, happy, and full of relief. "I would've picked you up myself. I'm so glad you're back."

Josephine waved Topher off, her eyes narrowing as she took in the chaotic scene unfolding around her. "The nurse you hired brought me back, and I'm glad she did because... what is all this?" She gestured toward the living room and kitchen, where ingredients were scattered on the counters, random equipment was piled up, and the tech guy was still crouched near the router. "I just got out of the hospital. I need peace, not a three-ring circus."

Topher smiled sheepishly. "We just tried to make sure everything was set up for you."

"Set up for what? A parade? I don't need a chef or whoever that is"—she pointed to the tech guy, who froze like a deer in headlights— "making a mess of my home. Everyone out! Now."

I bit my lip to keep from laughing as Topher scrambled to get everyone moving.

"Okay, okay, guys, you heard her. Time to go." He waved them out. The chef started packing up his gear, the tech guy scrambled to unplug something, and even the gardener was trying to escape quietly, broom still in hand.

The house emptied, and even the nurse, who had been lingering in the corner, left, though she promised she'd come back at least once a day. Josephine finally sank into her armchair with a relieved sigh, closing her eyes for a moment. "Now, we have something to discuss."

Topher and I exchanged puzzled looks.

"What's up?" Topher asked.

Josephine opened one eye, giving us a mischievous grin. "Now that I'm settled, we can talk about the next holiday. Halloween is coming up."

"Halloween?" Topher asked, raising an eyebrow. "Isn't it a bit early to worry about that?"

Josephine shook her head adamantly. "Oh no, it's never too early for Halloween. The entire neighborhood looks forward to my decorations. It's a tradition. And it's a contest."

"A contest?" I repeated, already feeling the pressure.

"Yes, and I've won five years in a row. I can't let the Hendersons take the title just because I'm under the weather this year," she said with a determined gleam in her eye.

Topher smirked. "So, you're saying the neighborhood won't survive a year without your Halloween display?"

"Precisely," Josephine said, her expression serious. "They rely on this house to set the bar. You can't just put out a couple of pumpkins and call it a day. It needs to be... spectacular."

Topher looked as uneasy as I felt. This wasn't going to be a small task.

"Well," I said hesitantly, "I guess we'll have to step up our game then."

Josephine nodded with satisfaction. "Good. Because if the Hendersons win, they'll never let me live it down."

Topher chuckled. "Alright, we'll make sure they don't steal your crown. But you're sure the neighborhood wouldn't let you take a year off?"

"Not a chance." Josephine looked exhausted all of a sudden. "I think I'm going to lie down for a few hours."

Topher's demeanor shifted instantly. He jumped to help her up from the chair. "Come on, let's get you into bed." He guided her gently toward the bedroom. His hands were steady, his touch gentle, as if every movement was made with her comfort in mind.

I lingered in the doorway, watching as he carefully settled his mom into bed.

"You're too good to me, Topher," she murmured as she patted his hand. She sighed, clearly exhausted but at peace, the lines on her face softening.

He smiled down at her, brushing a loose strand of hair from her face in such a tender gesture that it caught me off guard.

She patted his hand. "I've missed you. It's nice having you at home. Would you two make me dinner? Together?"

"I missed you, too," he said softly. "Now rest. We'll take care of dinner."

As he stood up to leave, she flashed one last small smile. "You always take care of everything, don't you?"

He chuckled lightly. "Not everything, but I'm learning."

A little tug pulled at my chest. There was a tenderness in Topher I hadn't expected—a side of him that showed how deeply he cared for his mom.

I never thought I could soften toward an annoyed, pampered, billionaire workaholic. But apparently miracles do happen.

9

It was official: the man who could manage a global empire couldn't manage a frying pan.

Teaching a billionaire to cook was going to be harder than I thought.

When I told Topher it was time to make dinner, he closed his laptop without protest, which was already shocking. However, he stared at the stove like it was a ticking bomb. "Just a heads-up... I don't cook. Ever. This could end in flames."

I blinked. "Wait, you've never made a meal in your life?"

Topher shrugged. "Well, before I had a chef, I was a master at PB&J and could microwave mac 'n' cheese like a pro. That counts, right?"

"If you think peeling the plastic off a cup of noodles qualifies as gourmet cooking, then sure. But today's your lucky day. You're about to discover that making a home-cooked meal can be fun."

Topher raised an eyebrow. "Fun? Yeah, I'll believe it when I see it."

"But before we start, you might want to change. Cooking in a suit isn't exactly a great idea."

He nodded, disappearing into the hallway. When he returned, I nearly dropped the spatula. Gone was the crisp suit that he looked so good in, replaced by an old, faded t-shirt that stretched across his chest and arms, hugging his torso just right. For a second, I forgot to breathe.

"Better?" he asked, completely unaware of the effect he was having on me.

I cleared my throat, trying to sound casual. "M-much better."

The house was so small it felt like there wasn't an inch of space to breathe without being in each other's way. It was clear that if we were going to survive this, we'd need to be on our best behavior at all times. No bickering, no snarky remarks. Which, given our constant state of verbal sparring, seemed nearly impossible. But with Josephine resting in her bedroom, the last thing we needed was her picking up on any tension between us.

As we got to work in the kitchen, I decided it was time to multi-task. "Alright, while we cook, I'm going to teach you some yoga poses to help you relax."

Topher frowned. "Yoga? I'm not exactly the flexible type."

I grinned. "You don't have to be a human pretzel. I'll just teach you a couple of simple poses that don't need much space. We can do them while we're waiting for the food to cook."

He gave me a dubious look. "So, I'm supposed to strike a pose in the middle of the kitchen?"

"Exactly. It's easier than you think. Just trust me, you'll feel better."

He looked at me like I was crazy, but went back to chopping vegetables. "Okay, enlighten me. How exactly is this going to help?"

"Because these poses are great for relaxing, and you can do them anytime or anywhere. Imagine this: a stressful board meeting, things aren't going your way—boom, you hit them with a Tree Pose."

"Tree Pose?"

"Watch." I stood on one leg, placing the other foot against my calf, and raised my arms above my head. "This is Tree Pose. It's all about balance. You try it, while I chop."

He raised an eyebrow but lifted one foot, wobbling as he balanced on the other. "This feels... unstable."

"Exactly!" I laughed. "Welcome to my world. Now focus. Find your center."

To my surprise, he actually tried. His face shifted from skepticism to concentration, and I could see him getting into it.

"Am I doing this right?"

"Not bad for a beginner. Now, let's try Warrior Pose. Take a wide stance, bend your front knee, and stretch your arms out. It's about feeling strong and grounded." I demonstrated, and he followed, though a bit clumsily.

"Strong and grounded, huh?" He looked at me sideways, but something about it must have clicked because he looked more relaxed. "Okay, I can see why this might be useful."

I smirked. "Told you. Now imagine doing this in the middle of a board meeting. Total power move."

"I don't think my board would know what hit them."

After that, he seemed more at ease, slicing the tomatoes with a jaw more relaxed than I'd ever seen it.

But then, when he was stirring a pot, his shoulders hunched, drawing up into his ears.

"Here, let me show you something." I stepped behind him and gently placed my hands on his shoulders, guiding them down and back. "Relax your shoulders, like this."

The moment my fingers made contact, a subtle jolt passed between us. He stiffened at first, but then melted into the touch, letting me ease the tension out of his muscles. His body was warm under my fingertips, and I could feel his breath catch before he exhaled.

"Better?" I tried to keep my voice steady, as if I wasn't suddenly hyper-aware of how close we were.

"Yeah," he murmured. "Better."

Trying to shake off the moment, I moved to the oven, focusing on the chicken as if it were the most fascinating thing in the world. Once it was grilled to perfection, I tossed it into the salad bowl and grabbed the vinaigrette.

"Alright, mix it all together." I handed him a spoon.

As the fresh, tangy smell of the vinaigrette filled the kitchen, I caught him giving the salad a slight, approving nod.

He shot me a begrudging smile. "Well, it's no protein shake, but I guess it'll do."

"Not bad for your first time."

For a moment, I forgot all the reasons why he usually drove me up the wall.

Just then, we heard Josephine call from the living room. "Is dinner ready?"

Topher and I quickly plated the salad and brought it over to the table. Together, we helped Josephine ease into her chair.

"So, Kathleen, what do you do for a living?" Josephine asked.

Topher raised an eyebrow, clearly interested in how I would handle this one.

"Oh, you know, a little bit of this, a little bit of that. You could say I'm still on the hunt for my dream job."

Josephine was intrigued. "So, what's the most memorable job you've had so far?"

"Well, there was this one time I worked at the DMV. I met so many interesting people. But I guess I was *too* friendly. They said I was making the experience *too* enjoyable for customers, so they let me go."

Josephine blinked. "Too enjoyable?"

"Yep. I became friends with the customers, which really annoyed my coworkers. I guess I was making the DMV experience 'too delightful.' That's a direct quote from my exit interview." I shrugged, and Topher burst out laughing.

Josephine grinned. "Well, that's a first. I've never heard of anyone being too delightful for the DMV."

"Oh, it gets better." I leaned in with a conspiratorial look. "I once tried telemarketing. You know, those calls no one likes getting? Well, turns out, I'm terrible at it. I was supposed to make a certain number of sales calls per hour, but I ended up just chatting with people. I didn't make a single sale."

Topher shook his head, clearly amused. "Not one sale?"

"Not one." I grinned. "They told me I was the worst telemarketer they'd ever had."

"Any other jobs?" Josephine prompted.

"Well, then there was a grocery store where I worked at a register, and I'd start talking with the customers. My lines ended up getting so long because I had my favorite people who kept coming back just to talk and to ask me for advice."

Topher leaned back in his chair, looking at me like he was seeing me for the first time. "You got fired from a grocery store for being too friendly?"

"Apparently, I was 'distracting from the core efficiency goals of the workplace,'" I said in my best bossy voice. "Which I think is just corporate-speak for 'too chatty.'"

Topher's expression lit up more than I'd ever seen, and Josephine was practically in tears from laughing.

"My dear," she said, dabbing her eyes, "you're a professional people person."

"I guess you're right." I couldn't help feeling a little proud of how much they were enjoying themselves. But then I glanced at Topher and felt a jolt—he was still looking at me. His gaze lingered just a second too long, and something fluttered in my chest before I could shut it down.

I looked away quickly, hoping his mom didn't notice the blush creeping up my neck.

As I finished talking (after mentioning my stints as a dog walker, barista, and cashier at a big-box store), Josephine jumped in with her own stories. It was surprisingly easy to keep up the fake-girlfriend charade.

After dinner, I cleaned the dishes and excused myself to the bedroom. A strange unease crept in. I wasn't supposed to be enjoying being part of this family dynamic and spending time with Topher and his mom. But I was. I shook off the thought and went to get my locket from my jewelry case, a small velvet pouch that had been through more moves than I cared to count.

Holding the locket always made me feel better, and I needed that comfort now.

But it wasn't there.

I tore through my suitcase, rifling through every piece of clothing, checking every pocket, even shaking out the case's lining. A lump was building in my throat. *Where was it?*

Frantic, I started pacing the room, scanning every corner, every surface. Maybe it had fallen out somewhere? Maybe it had gotten mixed up in the mess when I was unpacking. "No, no, no."

Topher walked into the room. "What's going on?"

"I can't find my locket!" My voice was shaky, barely holding it together. "It's gone. I've looked everywhere, and it's just... gone."

He stepped closer, his voice calm but serious. "What does it look like?"

I swallowed hard. "It's small, silver, heart-shaped. It has pictures of my parents inside."

Topher spoke authoritatively. "Let's retrace your steps."

We tore through the room together, checking every drawer, under the bed, even the closet, but nothing. I was starting to lose hope, my breath coming in short, uneven bursts. *It can't be gone. It just can't.*

"Maybe it's still at your old place," Topher suggested. "Let's call your landlord, see if he found it."

"Jerry?" I scoffed. "He probably won't answer."

Talking to Jerry would be pointless. He was the kind of guy who always had an excuse, a reason why something couldn't be done. My frustration with him had long since reached its limit.

"Leave it to me," Topher said, his voice confident as he took the phone from my hands. Miracle of all miracles, Jerry picked up after a few rings. Topher put the phone on speaker. "Hello, Jerry." Topher's voice was smooth but firm. "This is Topher Brodie. You might recognize the name. I'm with Kathleen Avery, and we're looking for a silver locket she left behind. Have you seen it?"

Jerry's response was predictably flat. "Nope, haven't seen anything like that. The place has already been taken by someone new. If Kathleen left her necklace behind, it's theirs now."

I slumped a little, biting my lip. Of course, Jerry would take the easy way out.

But Topher didn't flinch. "Jerry, I think you should understand the legal ramifications here. That locket is personal property left behind inadvertently. Under most property laws, you're responsible for making an effort to return it to the rightful owner."

There was a long pause, and I could almost picture Jerry's face, scrunched up in annoyance, trying to figure out how to wiggle out of this. "Look, I don't need a lesson in property law. The tenants have the place now, and I'm not going to get involved in your sob story."

Topher's grip on the phone tightened. "I'd advise you to reconsider that stance, Jerry."

Jerry let out an irritated sigh. "Look, I cleaned the place top to bottom and didn't find any necklace."

Topher's jaw tightened when he heard Jerry's story change. He was gearing up to argue again. This was a guy used to getting his way. "That's unaccept—"

"I said there's no necklace. Sorry." Jerry didn't sound sorry at all.

He ended the call, and a tear slipped down my cheek.

"It's lost. It's gone." I tried to hold it together, but the weight of losing the locket and all the uncertainty in my life hit me like a tidal wave. My chest tightened, and the tears fell faster.

Before I knew it, Topher had moved closer, his voice quiet and reassuring. "Hey, we'll get to the bottom of this. I promise." He reached out, gently pulling me into his arms, and I didn't resist. I couldn't. The sobs came, harder than I expected, and I buried my face into his chest, allowing him to hold me.

I cried, letting out everything I'd been bottling up, and as I did, a strange sense of relief washed over me. He didn't say anything, but just held me tighter, his hand rubbing small, soothing circles on my back.

For someone who was so bad at handling emotions, he was surprisingly good at making me feel better. As my sobs finally eased, I pulled away, feeling a strange mixture of embarrassment and relief. That's when it dawned on me: we had to sleep in the same room, and we still hadn't decided how the arrangement would work.

Topher gave me a small smile. "You okay?"

I wiped my eyes and nodded. "Yeah, but just to be clear, we're not sharing the bed."

Topher chuckled. "Kathleen, trust me. You couldn't pay me enough to sleep in the same bed with you."

"Hey!" I shot back. "That's supposed to be *my* line!"

He shrugged as if it were no big deal. "I'll make a Japanese bed on the floor."

I raised an eyebrow. "A Japanese bed?"

"Yeah. Thin mattress, no frame. I sleep better that way than in my expensive New York bed."

I blinked at him. "So... you've slept on the floor before?"

"Sure, at onsens in Japan."

I crossed my arms. "Well, I'm just warning you that I go to bed early. You'd better not stay up all night working."

"Can't make any promises." He smirked. "But I'll keep it quiet. We'll need to. Mom's room is right next door."

I groaned. "Great. Now I'll have to worry about being too loud when I toss and turn."

Topher guided me back to the living room, his hand warm and unexpected on my shoulder. "Just don't snore, and we'll be fine."

Later that night, after we'd gotten Josephine settled, the bedroom felt smaller than ever. Topher had set up his makeshift bed on the floor, and I was tucked under the covers of the double bed. He had a small desk light on, typing away on his laptop, while I attempted to get some sleep.

"Can you turn that off?" I asked, my voice muffled by the pillow.

"I'm almost done," he murmured, not looking up. "Just a few more things to finish."

"You're going to ruin your eyes," I muttered.

He reached into his bag and tossed something soft in my direction. "Here, use this."

It was an eye mask. "Thanks."

"Just trying to help." The faint glow of his laptop screen cast shadows across his face. As I glanced over, I could see him still looking at me, his expression softer than usual. "Thank you, by the way."

I blinked, taken aback. "For what?" I slid the mask over my eyes, my heart racing a little faster for reasons I didn't entirely understand.

"For getting my mind off worrying about my mom. She's really happy. I haven't seen her laugh like she did at dinner in a long time."

There was a quiet moment, and I guess neither of us felt we needed to fill the silence.

I pushed the mask off my eyes and noticed Topher absently rubbing his temples. Suddenly, Gladys's earlier comment about Topher's headaches came rushing back. A little twinge of concern stirred in my chest.

But then I gave in to the heaviness in my eyelids. "Goodnight, Topher."

"Goodnight, Kathleen."

As I lay there, I could still hear the faint tapping of his keyboard, but the soft eye mask blocked out the light.

And for the first time in a long time, I didn't feel so alone.

10

I WAS AWAKENED the next morning by the sound of groaning.

"Are you okay?" I rolled over to see Topher sprawled on the floor next to the bed.

"I didn't sleep at all," he grumbled, rubbing his back. "I feel like I've been run over by a truck."

"I thought you said you sleep better on the floor."

"Yeah, well, that's when the floor is in a Tokyo hotel with climate control and 800-thread count sheets." He sat up, stretching his arms above his head. "This... this is medieval torture."

His hair was a mess, and there were clear indentations on his cheek from the cushion he'd been using as a pillow. Frustratingly, it made him look even better—like some disheveled model in a magazine shoot.

Before I could say anything, he reached for his laptop. "I'll forget about it once I get into a work rhythm."

He clicked the power button, waited a few seconds, then blinked. "No. No way."

"What?" I already guessed the answer.

"The internet is down again!" He stared at his laptop like it had betrayed him. "I can't believe this."

"Why don't you just use your phone as a hotspot?"

He shook his head, his expression serious. "I can't risk it. For security reasons, my team has disabled hotspot capabilities on my devices. It's all to ensure that sensitive data doesn't get exposed over unsecured networks."

He stormed out of the room, and I followed him into the hallway, right in time to see his mom standing by the door, watching us both with a raised eyebrow.

"Morning," Josephine said, smiling softly. "Everything alright?"

"The internet's down again."

She shook her head and looked at him with a knowing smile. "You need to stop working so much."

Before Topher could open his mouth to argue, I jumped in, crossing my arms. "She's right. You need to stop working so much."

He shot me a sideways glance. "You're ganging up on me now?"

"Someone has to," I replied. "I mean, is the world going to fall apart if you take a day off?"

"The world? No. My company? Maybe."

Then he started barking orders into his phone. "Yeah, I need you over here, now. The Wi-Fi's out again." He paused. "I don't care if you had too much fun last night and are feeling it today."

When the tech guy showed up, he looked like he'd just crawled out of a New Orleans gutter. His clothes were rumpled, his eyes bloodshot, and the smell of stale alcohol clung to him. Clearly, he'd survived a wild night in the French Quarter.

"Let's just get this over with," Topher muttered.

The tech guy slumped down by the router, poking around with wires and muttering something under his breath. Finally, after what felt like forever, he stood up, wiping his forehead with the back of his hand.

"Well, the reason it was down is... a little odd." The tech guy scratched his head. "In the French Quarter, they say ghosts can mess with electronics. Maybe we've got a little supernatural interference?"

Topher shot him a flat look. "A ghost? Seriously?"

The tech guy shrugged. "Or, you know, just some local wiring interference. But it's fixed now."

Topher rubbed his temples. "Great. Thanks. Get some aspirin."

After the tech guy left, Josephine looked at us with a smile. "Why don't you both join me in the kitchen for a board game?"

I smiled at Josephine. "I'd love to. Let me get changed real quick."

Once the bedroom door clicked shut, I turned to Topher. "We really need to figure out this bedding situation."

We sat down in front of his laptop. "What about this blow-up mattress?" I asked.

Toper shook his head. "Look at the dimensions. There's no way that's fitting in the room."

"Wait, this looks comfortable. An inflatable beach lounger. It's in stock, and they have two-hour delivery if you pay extra."

Topher nodded. "That does look comfortable."

Once the order was placed, Topher was already making a beeline for his computer setup, clearly ready to dive back into his usual routine. "I've got things to take care of."

I stepped in front of him, blocking his path. "Oh no, you don't. Take a break, Topher. Spend a couple of hours with your mom. You won't get this time back."

He hesitated, glancing toward the kitchen where his mom sat at the table. I could see the internal struggle, the constant pull of his responsibilities that never seemed to let up.

"I do have stuff I need to finish." His eyes drifted toward his computer, as if it physically hurt to stay away from it.

"You can get back to it when she's napping. Trust me. A little break won't kill you."

He glanced at his mom again, and that's when I saw the moment she won. His shoulders slumped slightly, the tension easing just a fraction. "Alright, fine. But just for a little while."

I led him back into the living room, where Josephine had already set up a board game on the coffee table. It was *Scrabble*. Perfect for some lighthearted competition.

Topher's eyes lit up. "Now we're talking!"

Josephine grinned, giving him a playful nudge. "Topher loved this game as a kid. He used to beat all the adults."

"Of course I did," Topher said, practically bouncing into his seat. "It's been a while, but I'm ready to reclaim my title."

We started playing, and it didn't take long for Topher's competitive streak to kick into high gear. He was already eyeing the board like it was a chess match. Josephine, though, was no slouch, and she wasn't holding back, either.

"So, Topher," I asked with a grin, "did you really throw around words like 'ubiquitous' when you were eight?"

He flashed a smile. "I didn't just use 'ubiquitous.' I spelled it on a triple-word score."

Josephine laughed. "He was insufferable. The teachers didn't know what to do with him."

Topher smirked, not even denying it. "What can I say? I liked words."

"You mean, you liked showing off," I teased.

He laid down the word 'zodiac' on, predictably, a triple-word score. "Some things never change."

The game continued, and Josephine shared stories about how Topher would correct his teachers and successfully convince them to extend recess.

Josephine's laugh softened as she glanced at Topher, a flicker of worry crossing her face. "You were always so serious, even as a kid. Always concerned about things no child should have to worry about."

Topher's smile faded for a moment, his gaze dropping to the game board. "Well, someone had to keep things in order."

I felt a pang of curiosity and concern. What had happened when he was a kid? What could have made him feel so responsible, even back then? Whatever it was, its weight still seemed to cling to him.

The tension was palpable, and I could see the shadows of the past creeping back between them. I wanted to break the heaviness.

"Wait, wait," I said. "Are you telling me the same Topher Brodie who argues about the importance of work once argued for more recess?"

Topher's face broke into a sheepish smile, and Josephine's eyes twinkled as the mood lifted. "Yes," she said, chuckling. "He had a whole presentation—charts and everything."

Topher rolled his eyes, and I could see the tension ease from his shoulders. "What can I say? I've always been persuasive."

The doorbell rang, and my heart skipped a beat. Topher and I jumped up to answer it, and there stood Gladys, the nosiest neighbor in history, holding the massive box with the inflatable pool float and a suspicious look on her face.

"What's this?" she asked, raising an eyebrow, handing the box over to Topher.

Topher raised an eyebrow right back. "Are you a delivery driver now, Gladys?"

Gladys huffed, her hands on her hips. "I intercepted it! Thought it might be something interesting. So, what's the beach lounger for?"

Before Topher could answer, I blurted out, "It's, uh... for Halloween. We're doing a haunted beach theme this year."

Gladys looked intrigued. Then she winked at me. "A haunted beach, huh?"

I gave her my best *this-is-totally-normal* smile. "Yep! You know, spooky skeletons, surfboards... It's going to be... Scary."

Topher shot me a look that practically screamed, *Seriously? Spooky surfboards? That's what you're going with? Why not just tell her the pool floatie is for the pool at my mansion?* He quickly shoved the box behind the door, clearly trying to hide it before Gladys asked any more questions. "Anyway, thanks for bringing it over."

But Gladys, being Gladys, wasn't done. She pushed her way in, her curiosity far from satisfied. "A haunted beach. Josephine always comes up with the best decorations. I can't wait to see what you do this year."

Me too, Gladys, me too. I already dreaded figuring out how we'd pull this off.

"Oh, hello, Josephine, darling!" Gladys darted over to the kitchen and gave her a quick hug. "Scrabble, huh? I'll leave you three to it."

As soon as the door closed, Topher shook his head. "Gladys is so nosy. How do you put up with her?"

Josephine chuckled. "Gladys is just a caring neighbor."

Topher's voice dripped with sarcasm. "Caring? Sure, if you mean caring about being the first to spread gossip."

Josephine was unfazed. "She's harmless. Now, are we finishing this Scrabble game or not?"

We played a few games. Topher won them all by a landslide. Then, he and I headed to the kitchen to make lunch.

As I started chopping vegetables for a salad, Topher stirred the spaghetti sauce and slipped into a yoga pose. He had one leg stretched back in what I could only guess was Warrior, his other arm lazily swirling the spoon.

I paused, knife hovering above the cucumber. He had listened to me. Topher—the workaholic, always-on, never-slow-down Topher—was trying to relax. A sense of warmth spread through me.

After lunch, Josephine rested most of the day, allowing Topher plenty of time to work. Later that night, after we'd cleaned up dinner and Josephine had gone to bed, it was time to set up Topher's bed.

"How hard could this be?" He ripped the box open.

I eyed the lounger. "So...do we have a plan for blowing this thing up?"

After scouring the house for an air pump and coming up empty, we realized we'd have to inflate it the old-fashioned way. Lung power. We each took a valve and started blowing. Within minutes, I was lightheaded, and Topher wasn't faring any better.

"This...is...ridiculous," I gasped, pausing to catch my breath. "Why...didn't we...get the next size...down?"

Topher, equally out of breath, just laughed between puffs. "Who...knew...blowing up...a beach lounger...was...an Olympic sport?"

After several dizzying rounds of huffing and puffing, the lounger was finally inflated. We collapsed onto the now-bouncy surface, panting and laughing like we'd just finished a marathon.

"You know," Topher said, "I'm not sure if it's the exhaustion talking, but this is way more comfortable than it has any right to be."

"So," I said, turning to face him, "when was the last time you had to blow something up manually?"

Topher let out a small chuckle. "Does my ego count?"

Well, well, well, Topher Brodie making fun of himself. I raised an eyebrow, feeling a grin spread across my face. "If it did, I think we'd need a lot more than lung power."

He gave a half-smile, his tone shifting slightly. "You joke, but honestly, I might have a big ego for a reason. With some of the decisions I have to make, it's necessary."

I blinked, caught a little off guard. "Oh, please. What could be stressful about choosing between fifty different shades of navy-blue suits?"

"You'd be surprised," he replied with mock seriousness, his eyes twinkling. "Do you know how many variations of navy exist? It's a minefield."

I snorted. "Your life is truly a hardship. What's next? You can't decide which luxury watch to wear?"

Topher placed a hand over his heart, leaning into the joke. "The struggle is real. Too much gold, not enough platinum. It's a nightmare."

I laughed. "I'm sure."

We kept talking, the conversation flowing effortlessly. Somehow, between the jokes and playful jabs, I found myself relaxing even more. It was easy to forget, just for a little while, that we were supposed to be pretending to be something we weren't.

But then, as I shifted on the lounger, I noticed something strange. The surface beneath me was slowly sinking.

"Topher," I whispered, nudging him with my elbow. "The beach lounger's dying."

He glanced down, and for a moment, he just stared at the deflating palm trees. Then, much to my surprise, he started laughing. Deep, genuine laughter that made his eyes crinkle at the corners. "You've got to be kidding me."

I groaned. "All that work was wasted. Come on, we've got to find something else for you."

We tiptoed through the house, gathering every cushion and blanket we could find. Soon, we fashioned a makeshift bed on the floor, layering it with everything soft we could gather. Topher lay down, testing it with a satisfied sigh.

"Not bad." He flashed me a grin as I climbed into the bed.

I smiled back. "At least you won't wake up feeling like you've been run over by a truck."

As I lay in bed, the tension in the air slowly dissolved. The guy who seemed to thrive on pressure, who I was convinced hadn't taken a real break in years, was starting to unwind.

And then, to my surprise, I heard the unmistakable sound of his breathing slowing as he fell asleep. Topher Brodie, the man who probably considered sleep an inconvenience, who once boasted about only needing four hours a night, had dozed off... before me.

11

TOPHER LOOKED RIDICULOUSLY happy in his sleep, sprawled on the floor in the morning light with a blanket half-draped over him, like he was dreaming of closing the biggest deal of his life.

It was hard to stay irritated when he looked so adorable. All his sharp edges and arrogance were softened, and he looked kind of cute. Of course, I'd never tell him that. The moment he woke up, he'd be back to his usual, all-business self. But for now? Yeah, he was pretty much impossible to hate.

I slipped out of the room and headed toward the kitchen, where I could already hear the faint sound of classic rock. I wasn't prepared for what I found.

There was Josephine, in her bright floral robe, quietly *grooving* around the kitchen, her hips swaying to the Rolling Stones' "Start Me Up" playing on low volume. In one hand, she held a spatula; in the other, a frying pan, as she danced her way from the stove to the fridge and back again.

"Good morning, sunshine!" she said in a whisper-shout, throwing in a little hip shimmy as she flipped an omelet. "Topher still asleep?"

"Yeah. You're having way too much fun for this hour."

"Honey, if you're not moving, you're not living." She gave the spatula a quick flip. "Alexa, keep it low."

"*Volume at a respectful level,*" Alexa responded in its usual robotic tone, which made me chuckle.

"You've trained her well," I teased.

Josephine winked. "Oh, I run a tight ship. She knows not to mess with me, especially not before coffee."

She gave a little twirl as she whisked the eggs, her moves as fluid as someone half her age. I watched her, wondering where this woman found her energy so soon after leaving the hospital. "Should you be cooking right now?"

Josephine waved off my concern as if it were nothing. "Of course I should! You know, when Topher was a kid, I used to cook for him every morning. He could eat his weight in pancakes." She smiled, the kind of warm, mischievous smile that made you feel like you were in on some kind of inside joke. Despite everything she'd been through, she looked happy. Stronger than yesterday.

Josephine held up a spatula, pointing it toward me like a microphone.

"Now, what'll it be? Rock star omelets or scrambled eggs with a side of disco?"

"An omelet sounds great but let me help you."

Josephine smiled, gave a little twirl, and winked. "Omelets it is. And you can help me by sitting and talking to me." She grinned as she cracked an egg into the pan, then grabbed a second plate and set it down in front of me without asking, as if it was the most natural thing in the world, like I belonged there. A warm, fuzzy feeling spread through me.

But almost instantly, I felt guilty. This was all fake. Pretending to be close to Topher, playing the doting girlfriend. It wasn't real. And the better I got to know Josephine, the worse I felt deceiving her.

As she flipped the omelet, I glanced at her. "You know, Topher told me he'd love for you to move closer to him. But you seem so happy here. What is it about New Orleans that makes you stay?"

Josephine paused, a soft smile crossing her face. "Oh, I know. Topher's always trying to get me to move. But this city has got a hold on me. There's just something about it. It's hard to put into words."

"I get that," I said, leaning forward. "What do you love most about it?"

She flipped the omelet with ease. "It's the rhythm, the people, the places. I've been here for years, and it's always felt like home. There's a certain magic to New Orleans. You find your spots, your routines, and they become part of your life."

I nodded. "It's like every corner of the city has a story, something special."

She smiled, her eyes lighting up. "Exactly! That's what I've tried to create at Muses—a place where everyone is welcome. And there's this little coffee shop I love a few blocks over. It's called Brewed Awakening. I used to go there all the time when I needed to step away from everything. The regulars are like family, the baristas know your name, and it's just a comfortable place."

"That sounds wonderful."

She plated the omelets and sat down across from me, smiling. "Maybe Brewed Awakening will become one of your spots, too. Plus, they give out free muffins."

I laughed. "Now you're speaking my language." As she plated the omelets, I couldn't help but glance at her more closely. "You seem to be feeling better today."

"Oh, I am," she said, setting a plate in front of me. "You and Topher have been a big help, you know."

Speaking of Topher, I leaned back in my chair, trying to sound casual. "You ever notice how he's *always* working? Like, constantly?"

Josephine sighed, sitting down across from me. "That boy doesn't know how to slow down. He's got the weight of the world on his shoulders. Like if he stops for even a second, everything will fall apart."

I nodded, my heart giving a little squeeze. I didn't know why I cared so much about his well-being, but there it was. "He acts like the world will collapse if he's offline for five minutes."

Josephine tried to hide her grin, but it slipped out. "Well, the internet *does* tend to get a little... spotty when he's home."

I stared at her, something clicking into place. "Wait a second. Have you been messing with the Wi-Fi?"

Josephine gasped, her hand flying to her chest in an overly dramatic display. "Me? Sabotage my own son's internet? Never!" But the twinkle in her eye gave her away.

I crossed my arms, raising an eyebrow. "You have, haven't you?"

She sighed, dropping the act with a guilty smile. "Alright, fine. I might've unplugged a thing or two here and there. But in my defense, he works too much! A little break won't kill him."

I remembered the weird episode with Gladys and the Saran Wrap in the kitchen. "Did you get Gladys in on this scheme too?"

Josephine's eyes sparkled with mischief. "She was a *very* willing participant. You know how much she loves getting into people's business."

I shook my head but smiled. "You're devious."

She grinned. "Please don't tell Topher, though. It's been so good to see him relax."

"So, that's your grand plan? Sabotage his Wi-Fi, so he'll slow down?"

Josephine chuckled, a little too pleased with herself. "It's worked so far, hasn't it?" She gave me a knowing smile, her eyes twinkling. "You're good for him. Whether he admits it or not."

Just then, Topher walked into the kitchen, his brown hair perfectly mussed, as handsome as I had ever seen him. He crossed the room with that easy stride of his and bent down to kiss his mother on the cheek. "How are you doing?"

"Better every day, sweetie," she said.

Topher swept across the kitchen and wrapped his arm around my waist. "Good morning, beautiful." His sleep-roughened voice made me want to melt, but his strong arm kept me upright as he pulled me closer. "I'm the luckiest man alive." Before I could respond, he leaned in and gently brushed a strand of hair behind my ear. "You always manage to look perfect in the morning."

I blinked. "Perfect? I didn't even brush my hair."

He grinned, leaning just a little closer. "Well, whatever you're doing, it's working." I could feel my face heat up, and before I could come up with a response, he added, "Is it some secret moisturizer or something? Because you're glowing."

I blinked again, dazed. "Uh, coconut oil... I guess?"

Topher chuckled softly, his voice low and teasing, his breath warm against my skin. "Coconut oil. Noted. Whatever it is, don't ever stop."

The warmth in his voice, the way his hand rested on my waist, and how he looked at me like I was the only thing that mattered.

"I won't," I said, barely thinking before speaking, "if it keeps you this close." Butterflies stirred in my stomach.

He looked at me with such intensity, such warmth. His touch sent a little thrill through me, his smile making my heart stumble in my chest. I reached up and pushed a wayward strand of hair off his forehead, smiling.

"Oh, you two." His mom laughed. "Nothing like young love, is there?"

Reality hit, hard and fast, like a cold splash of water.

All for show. His mother was there. This was all part of the charade, part of the lie we were selling. But for a moment, it had felt real, as if he were a man in love. My body had responded before my brain could catch up, leaning ever so slightly into his touch, craving more of the connection I hadn't realized I wanted.

I felt a pang of sadness, a heaviness in my chest, knowing that it was fake.

Still, for just a moment, it had felt nice. Really nice.

Josephine looked between the two of us, her smile wide. "So, what made you fall for Kathleen?"

Topher paused, his arm tightening just slightly around my waist.

For a second, I wondered if he'd been caught off guard. Then, as if he'd just thought of the funniest thing in the world, he grinned.

"Well, I couldn't resist the way she almost mowed me down with a shuttle at the airport. Most women give me their number, but Kathleen? She tried to give me whiplash."

Josephine laughed, and it was a full, joyful sound. Topher was good at this.

"And the way she yelled at me afterwards? That sealed the deal." His voice was light, teasing, but with just the right amount of sincerity. "I thought, 'Here's a woman who's not afraid to put me in my place.' People don't do that to me too often. They tiptoe around everything. But not Kathleen."

He smoothed my hair, flashing a crooked grin that made my stomach flip. "I was a goner right from the start."

Josephine turned to me. "And what about you? What made you fall for my son?"

I nearly choked on the air I was breathing. "Fall for him?" I stalled for a moment, wracking my brain. "Well, he's tall, so he can always reach things on the top shelf, which is handy. And, he's like a human encyclopedia. Doesn't matter what the topic is. He always has an answer. He's probably right ninety percent of the time, but believe me, he never doubts that other ten percent."

Josephine clapped her hands, laughing. "Yes, yes! Exactly! He *always* thinks he knows everything!"

Topher rolled his eyes, clearly outnumbered. "Hey, I'm right at least ninety-*five* percent of the time! You two are just ganging up on me."

I grinned. "See? He can't help himself. It's part of his charm."

But then I paused, my voice softening. "I think it's how he drops everything for the people he loves. Like the way he came to New Orleans when he found out you were sick. And the way he looks at you in the hospital, as if nothing else in the world matters. I saw how he was completely overwhelmed, but he still tried to act calm for your sake. And I remember thinking... that's the kind of person you want in your corner. Someone who shows up when it counts, even if they don't know how to say it."

Topher's eyes flicked to mine, surprised and pleased. However, the moment was over almost as quickly as it had happened.

My phone buzzed loudly on the table. I glanced down, my stomach flipping again, but for entirely different reasons this time.

The loan company. Again.

I could feel the color drain from my face, and I was desperately trying to hide my anxiety. "I, uh, I need to take this. I'll be right back." I hurried outside, my heart pounding in my chest.

When I was out of sight, I answered the call, my hands shaking. The voice on the other end was cold and impersonal, reminding me of overdue payments and accruing interest. The weight of my debt pressed down on me like a heavy stone.

I tried to keep my voice calm, but the panic was rising. "I know... I just need more time. Please."

After the call ended, I stood there, my back against the house, trying to steady my breathing. My hands trembled, and my mind raced. I needed a plan. I needed to fix this, but I wasn't sure how.

Suddenly, I felt a presence behind me. Topher had followed me outside.

"Are you okay?" His voice was soft but full of concern.

I straightened, quickly trying to pull myself together. "Yeah, just financial stuff. It's nothing I can't handle."

His brows furrowed, and he took a step closer. "If you need help—"

"No," I cut him off, sharper than I intended. "I don't need your help. I've got this."

There was a beat of silence before I turned away, desperate to escape his concerned gaze. "I just need to clear my head. I'll be fine."

Without warning, Topher stepped forward and wrapped his arms around me, pulling me into a hug. His embrace was warm and firm, and I could feel the steady beat of his heart against my back.

I blinked in surprise. "Why are you hugging me?"

He leaned in, his voice low in my ear. "Just go with it. My mom's watching."

But something about the way he held me felt different. His heart was racing at first, his chest rising and falling a little too fast. Slowly, I felt him relax, his grip softening as if he was holding me not for show but because he wanted to.

I didn't pull away.

His hand stroked gently up my back, and I closed my eyes, letting the comfort of his touch wash over me. I could feel his nose nuzzle my ear when he whispered, "Everything will work out. I promise."

For a moment, it was like the world had disappeared, and all that was left was the steady rhythm of his breath, the warmth of his body, and the way he wove our fingers together and then tucked a loose strand of hair behind my ear.

It was fake. I knew that.

But it felt real.

And I couldn't help but wonder if, for just a second, Topher felt it, too.

12

TODAY WAS THE DAY: the one I'd been dreading.

We were decorating for Halloween. A *beach-themed* Halloween because that's what I'd blurted out to Gladys.

Naturally, Topher was nowhere to be found. When I woke up, he was already gone. For a brief, startling moment, I realized I missed him.

Not the arguing, not the workaholic intensity, but waking up and seeing him there. His hair slightly mussed, his breathing steady and soft. When he opened his eyes and caught me watching, he'd give me a quiet, sleepy smile.

Now, with him gone, the space felt too still. Too wide.

I didn't have to wait long for an explanation. He came back just as I was finishing a late breakfast, carrying his laptop under one arm. When I asked where he'd been, he shrugged.

"Internet here's too spotty. Had to go to my place in the Garden District. People are relying on me. I can't just take off for a week." There was something almost sincere in the way he said it. I still thought he was overdoing it, but I could see the weight of his responsibilities in his face.

"Don't you trust the people working for you?" I asked.

Topher sighed, setting his laptop down and rubbing his temples like he always did when something frustrated him. "Some of the people I work with... they're cutthroat. You give them an inch, and they'll take your company. It's not exactly a relaxing environment."

Whoa. That was a side of him I hadn't seen before. *Just how bad were things behind the scenes?*

"But"—Topher leaned casually against the doorframe—"I'm done working for the day. And now I'm ready to decorate this yard for Halloween like it's never been decorated before." There was a mischievous glint in his eye.

He disappeared into the bedroom, and when he came back, I nearly dropped the cup of coffee in my hands.

Topher Brodie—Mr. Buttoned-Up Billionaire—was wearing a Hawaiian shirt.

Well, *barely* wearing one.

The top half hung open, revealing part of his chest. I blinked. Was it hot in here? Had the air conditioning stopped working? Oh boy.

"What on earth are you wearing?" I asked, barely hiding my inner spiral.

He looked down, as if noticing the palm trees and flamingos splashed across the fabric. Then he looked back at me with a slow, smug grin. "It's a beach-themed Halloween. Gotta commit, right?"

I raised an eyebrow, trying not to stare. I failed. "Who *are* you, and what have you done with Topher?"

He smirked. "Just go with it. It's going to be a long day."

He wasn't wrong.

As soon as we stepped outside, Topher was in full-on "boss mode." He waved his phone around like he was leading a battalion. "I've already called in my team." He scrolled through an absurdly long list of Halloween items. "We're getting everything delivered: haunted tiki bars, zombie surfers, skeleton lifeguards."

His "team," as I learned, was a mix of people from his mansion across town in the Garden District—gardeners, contractors, and his tech guy. Of course, these people weren't just helping out because it was fun. They were the best money could buy, and it showed.

I raised an eyebrow. "How much are you spending on this?"

Topher shrugged, entirely unbothered. "Whatever it takes. No limits."

Of course. Why would a billionaire have a budget for a Halloween beach display?

Within a couple of hours, we had transformed the yard into what can only be described as a haunted beach nightmare. A skeleton lifeguard stood tall on its perch, sunglasses on, a whistle dangling around its neck, guarding the yard with a sign that read, *"No Swimming: Sharks."*

Meanwhile, Topher and I were debating the number of zombie surfers.

"We need at least four more," he insisted.

"Four more? We've already got four!"

"You can never have too many undead surfers," he said with a grin, like it was some universal truth.

He was having fun. Real fun. Not the half-smile he gave during a work victory or the smirk when he made a sarcastic comment. No, this was genuine. And it was nice to see him like this. Josephine, who had come out to watch, seemed to love it, her face lighting up every time Topher added something over the top to the display.

I busied myself setting up several gravestones in the sand. Beach chairs and umbrellas were surrounded by gravestones with phrases like *"Here Lies my Beach Body, Never Found"* and *"Sunburned to Death."* Topher had suggested adding *"Gone Fishing... Forever."*

The real showstopper, though, was the Haunted Tiki Bar. An animatronic skeleton bartender was set up to serve spooky cocktails.

And then there was the sandcastle graveyard. Topher's gardeners, who I was now convinced could build anything, had created a towering sandcastle under a tarp in the yard, surrounded by tiny gravestones. A skeleton hand poked out from the top, looking like it was trying to escape.

"You sure this isn't too much?" I asked, stepping back to take it all in.

"We're not even done," Topher said, holding up a string of screaming seashells his tech guy had rigged. The seashells were set to let out eerie wails whenever someone walked by. "What do you think? Too creepy?"

"Too creepy? No." I shook my head. "Too ridiculous? Absolutely."

Josephine was beaming from the porch, clearly in love with the whole spectacle. Her pride in Topher was evident, and I couldn't help but feel warm inside. He could've just paid people to build the display, but instead, he was taking a major role, running around like a man on a mission, and it was hard not to admire that.

Just when I thought things couldn't get more absurd, Gladys strolled up.

"Well, well, well," she chirped, her eyes scanning the yard with a mix of awe and judgment. "Looks like somebody's trying to win the award for the most money spent on a yard."

Before I could jump in, Josephine appeared beside me, her grin wide. "Gladys, isn't it fabulous? The whole neighborhood will be talking about it by the time Halloween rolls around!"

Gladys blinked. "Well, it's certainly... *different*."

"Different is good," Topher said. "That's what we were going for."

Josephine beamed and turned to Gladys with a smile. "Why don't you come inside? We can chat over some tea."

As they disappeared into the house, probably planning to dissect every last detail of our Halloween extravaganza, I turned back to Topher, feeling a mix of exasperation and amusement.

"Okay, you can admit it now," I said, crossing my arms. "We've officially gone overboard."

He grinned, adjusting his Hawaiian shirt with a sense of pride. "Nah, if anything, we're just getting started."

I tried not to laugh. "You're insane."

"Maybe," he replied, glancing over at the sandcastle graveyard with a satisfied look. "But admit that you love it."

And as much as I hated to admit it, he was right. Watching him take charge, fully committed to making this ridiculous project a reality, made me see him in a new light. I had to hand it to him. Topher knew how to go all out, and it was kind of impressive.

But my admiration was short-lived. I reached across the tiki bar to fix a crooked skull garnish, and my elbow sent a very real, very full fishbowl cocktail flying. Straight into my shirt. Fantastic.

Cursing under my breath, I darted inside to change. Jeans and a t-shirt felt too stifling in this heat. The day had gotten unbearably hot, even for early October, and with the sun beating down, the idea of putting on anything heavy seemed like a punishment. So, I reached for the one thing that sounded comfortable: a simple sundress I rarely wore.

When I came back out, Topher's eyes widened. He paused, his gaze lingering just long enough to make me feel unexpectedly flattered.

"Nice outfit," he said, a hint of surprise in his voice.

A slight blush crept up my cheeks, but I brushed it off, adjusting the dress. "Thanks. It was either this or passing out from heatstroke in jeans."

He nodded, still watching me with a half-smile that made my stomach do a weird little flip.

Just then, I felt something soft and stringy brushing against my arm.

I froze. Slowly, I glanced down, and there it was. A giant, sticky spider web was draped all over my arm and stuck to the back of my dress.

"Oh my GOSH, it's ON ME!" I screamed, leaping into the air like I'd been hit with a taser. I flailed wildly, arms pinwheeling, trying to shake off the web that seemed to be growing by the second. "GET IT OFF!"

Topher stared at me for a split second before bursting into laughter. "It's just—"

"IT'S A SPIDER!" I shrieked, now hopping around like I was

dodging landmines. "I CAN FEEL IT CRAWLING!" I was spinning in circles, slapping my own back like a lunatic.

Topher was doubled over at this point, tears in his eyes. "It's a fake spider *web*, not an actual spider! You're fighting Halloween decorations!"

I stopped mid-spin, still slapping at my shoulder. "Are you SURE? Because I'm about two seconds away from setting myself on fire to make sure it's gone."

He was laughing so hard he could barely breathe. "Trust me," he wheezed, "if it were real, it wouldn't survive how fast you're moving."

I glared at him, trying to muster some dignity, but the web still clung to me like it had a vendetta. "I swear, this thing is multiplying!" I yanked at it, only managing to stick it to my other arm, which made Topher laugh even harder.

Still chuckling, he started untangling me. "Hold still before you knock over the tiki bar."

I stopped long enough to glare at him. "This isn't funny!"

He stepped closer, still grinning like he couldn't help it. "Oh, it's funny."

"Okay, maybe it's a little funny," I admitted. Every nerve seemed to hum as his fingertips brushed against my back. His touch was light, barely there, but enough to make my breath hitch. The warmth of his body so close sent a strange tingle through me. I couldn't help but think of the hug earlier.

I swallowed, trying to shake off the feeling. "But I swear, if there's an actual spider—"

"There's not," he said softly, pulling the last of the web from my shoulder. His fingers lingered for just a second too long, and my skin seemed to buzz where he touched me. "You're safe."

I huffed, straightening my sundress, pretending his closeness didn't completely throw me off. "Great. The spiderwebs win this round."

Topher's eyes were still sparkling with amusement.

"I'm glad *one* of us is having fun," I said, crossing my arms in mock indignation, though the smile tugging at my lips ruined the effect. "You know, you've been smiling a lot more these days."

He raised an eyebrow. "I never smile."

"Oh, really?" I shot back, raising my own eyebrow. "Because you're smiling right now."

He paused, as if he were genuinely contemplating this. "No, I'm not."

I pointed at his face, leaning in. "Uh, yeah, you are. Right there. The corners of your mouth? They're betraying you."

He gave a small huff, pretending to be annoyed. His gaze met mine, and for a moment, something shifted in the air between us. Then, to my surprise, he quietly said, "Because of you."

The words were so simple, yet they landed with an unexpected weight. It was like he hadn't planned on saying it, and once it slipped out, we were both left blinking at each other.

"Wait," I said, holding up my hands, "*I* make you smile?"

"Apparently," he muttered, rubbing the back of his neck.

"Well, now I feel powerful." I grinned, crossing my arms again. "I can make *Topher Brodie* smile. Should I add that to my résumé?"

He shook his head, chuckling despite himself. "Don't let it go to your head."

"Oh, it's too late for that," I teased.

He shot me a look, but there was no denying the smile that crept in again. "You're ridiculous."

"And yet," I said, my grin widening, "you're still smiling."

He gave up, letting the full smile break through. "Yeah. I guess I am. Actually, I've been doing some of those relaxation exercises you suggested. And, you know, they're helping. That and the sleep... my headaches are getting better."

"Really? That's great."

Topher nodded. "I guess you're good for me."

His words landed softly, but they struck me. My heart skipped a beat. *Good for him?* I scrambled to respond and could feel a slight flush creeping up my neck, my pulse quickening in a way that surprised me. Was he serious? Was this still part of the whole fake relationship thing?

There was a part of me that wanted to freeze the moment and examine every piece of it. But another part, the one I wasn't quite ready to admit to, wanted to savor it.

Pull it together, I reminded myself. This was just Topher being... *friendly*, right?

But before I could dwell on it, I remembered something I'd heard about recently, a perfect diversion. "Hey, speaking of good... I heard about this great cause. They're raising money for a foundation called Bright Futures. It provides scholarships to kids who've lost their parents. Helps them get an education without being buried under student loans."

Topher scoffed, shattering the softer moment. "Scholarships? Why not teach them how to invest early on? That would have more of a lasting impact than just handing them money for tuition."

I rolled my eyes, the warm feeling from before evaporating as quickly as it had come. *Of course.* Just when I thought I saw a decent side of him, he doubled down on being an uncaring jerk. "You wouldn't just be handing out money. It's an application process: deserving students would have to apply and be chosen."

"Giving away money doesn't solve anything," he said, his voice slipping into that too-familiar, business-like tone. "It just creates dependency."

I shot him a look. "You think everything's about investments and returns."

Topher paused, maybe realizing he'd gone too far, and ran a hand through his hair. "Okay, maybe I didn't say that right." His tone shifted. "It's not that I don't think scholarships matter. I just... I think there's more we can do to help people long term, you know? Set them up for real success."

I blinked, surprised. For once, it didn't feel like he was talking down to me.

I relaxed a little, my irritation fading. "It's not just handing out money. It's giving people a chance, giving them that first step." I smiled and paused. "Kind of like how *you* need someone like me to help you smile. Some kids need that same kind of help to get through school and have a shot at a future without being buried in debt."

Topher looked at me closely, a flicker of something almost concerned in his eyes. "Is this about you?" His voice was softer now, without the usual edge.

The question caught me off guard, and before I could stop myself, the words started pouring out. "It's not *about* me, but I know what it feels like. You have these dreams, all these plans for your life, but then the bills pile up, and suddenly you can't breathe. It starts to feel like no matter how hard you push, you're just stuck. Like your dreams are slipping away."

I wasn't sure why I was opening up like this, but I couldn't seem to stop. Despite all my rules, all the walls I'd built to keep anyone from getting too close, the words kept coming. Maybe it was the way he was looking at me. Like he wasn't judging, like he *understood*. "Sometimes it feels like no matter how hard I push, I'm just running in place. I start to wonder if I'll ever catch up, if it's even possible to get ahead. Or if I'm just destined to fall short, over and over again."

I could have told him everything in that moment—about the debt, about my parents. The words were right there on the tip of my tongue. For the first time, I felt like I could *trust* someone with the mess that was my life. Like he might understand and not look at me differently.

But before I could say another word, the sound of hurried footsteps on the porch made us both turn.

Gladys rushed out, her face pale, her voice trembling. "It's your mom. She collapsed."

13

IT PAYS TO HAVE A CHAUFFEUR. But it *really* pays when that chauffeur happens to be a war-trained driver who can weave through traffic like he's dodging landmines. And it's especially helpful when your body-guard is trained in first aid and immediately starts working on your mother in the backseat.

While Topher's assistant called ahead to make sure a room was ready, the car raced through the city. Forget waiting for an ambulance. We got to the hospital in record time.

As soon as we arrived, Topher's mother was whisked into a hospital room. Topher and I were all alone in the waiting room, the hospital eerily quiet. Topher sat beside me, staring down at his hands.

I shifted in my seat. "You know, she's got a lot of strength. Whatever happens, she's not the type to give up easily."

Topher exhaled, still not looking up. "Yeah, I know."

There was a pause before I added gently, "It's okay to feel worried, though."

He hesitated, his gaze still fixed on his hands. "I'm not worried." The crack in his voice made it clear he wasn't convincing either of us.

I waited, sensing there was more beneath the surface. After a moment, he glanced up at me briefly before looking back down, his posture rigid. "My mom..." His voice was low and uncertain, like he wasn't sure if he should be saying anything at all. "When she was raising me, she did everything she could, you know? Worked multiple jobs and always made sure I had something to eat, even when she didn't. But it wasn't enough. We were poor. 'Electricity-getting-shut-off' poor. 'Not-knowing-where-you're-going-to-sleep' poor."

His words hung in the air, and their weight hit hard as the tension built in his face. "It all started after my dad left. He completely disappeared. And then it was just the two of us, struggling every single day. We lost our house."

"That must have been hard for both of you." I kept my tone gentle, letting him know it was safe to keep talking.

He sighed, running a hand through his hair. "It was. We stayed in cheap motels, sometimes in the car. My mom tried to make it seem like an adventure, but I knew, even as a kid, I knew how close we were to losing everything. I had to drop out of school for a while to help her make ends meet."

"You dropped out of school?" I tried to keep the shock out of my voice, but my heart ached at the thought of him, a kid, giving up his education to survive. "How old were you?"

"Twelve," he replied, his eyes distant, as if he were looking back at a version of himself he hadn't thought about in a long time.

"That's such a young age to go through something so painful."

He nodded, clearing his throat. "Yeah. I lied about my age and worked whatever jobs I could. I bagged groceries and delivered papers. It was hard. But we made it. Eventually, we scraped enough together to get a tiny apartment. I went back to school, and I got a scholarship to pay for it. And my mom saved every penny. That's why she's so proud of her little house. She bought it herself."

He nodded, his face tightening. "There was no one. No friends offering money. No family swooping in to save the day. We had to help ourselves."

"That must have felt isolating," I said softly. "Like you had no choice but to grow up faster than anyone should have to."

"Yeah. And I promised myself I'd never be that powerless again. Never let her, or myself, go through that again."

As his words settled between us, my heart twisted. Even as a kid, he'd been so resilient, so strong. "You were carrying so much, even at twelve. That must have been incredibly difficult. And now you've built so much."

He gave a small, humorless laugh, but I could see a hint of pride beneath the pain. "Yeah. I guess so."

"And now you're working like you can never stop because you're still trying to make sure you never lose everything again."

He looked up at me, his eyes filled with something unspoken, as if he hadn't fully realized that himself. "Yeah," he admitted after a pause. "I can't stop. It's like... if I stop, if I let go for even a second, everything could fall apart. No matter how many houses I own or how many deals I close, it's always there. The fear. The pressure."

Topher's face changed. The tough exterior he'd been holding onto slipped, just a little. Worry flickered in his eyes. "What if... what if I lose her?"

Without thinking, I reached out and took his hand. No one was around to see it. There was no audience, so there was no reason to pretend. But in that moment, I didn't let go.

His grip tightened around my hand, and we sat there for a while, just like that.

Eventually, he shifted closer to me, his hand still in mine. He glanced up, and there was something softer in his gaze. He studied me for a moment. "You really are something." His voice was low, sincere. "You talk to people. You make them feel better. You should do that for a living."

I blinked, caught off guard. No one had ever said something like that to me, and for a moment, I didn't know how to respond. "I *do* need to get a real job. I was thinking, I don't know, maybe I'll work at a movie theater or something."

He raised an eyebrow. "A movie theater? Come on, you should be doing something that lets you connect with people, something that matters. Like being a therapist."

"A therapist?" I scoffed. "I can't afford a decade of school. I haven't even finished college."

I had so much debt, so many reasons why this wasn't possible. Yet, looking at him, I saw how open and sincere he was, and I felt something inside me soften. Maybe he wasn't as far removed from my struggles as I'd thought.

Sure, he was a billionaire, living in a world of luxury I could hardly imagine, but he hadn't always been that way. He'd known the weight of poverty, the gnawing uncertainty of whether tomorrow would be any better than today.

I could see it now, the way his workaholism wasn't about the need to pay bills anymore; it was deeper than that. It was the trauma of knowing what it felt like to have nothing and the fear that it could all slip away again. He wasn't just driven by ambition; he was driven by the same fear that haunted me, the same insecurity that gnawed at the back of my mind. But while I was still stuck in the fight to survive, he was on the other side of it, clinging to what he had built as if it could vanish any second.

We weren't as far apart as I'd thought. We were both shaped by the same fear, though his manifested in relentless work and mine in constant worry. Maybe, just maybe, we understood each other more than I'd ever imagined.

He looked deep in my eyes, and for a moment, I forgot how to breathe. My heart pounded so loudly in my ears that I was sure he could hear it, too. There was something in his eyes, something warm and steady that made me feel like the whole world had narrowed down to just the two of us.

Topher's gaze lingered, his face inches from mine, and I swore he was about to lean in. My pulse quickened, and heat rose in my cheeks. Was this really about to happen? Were we going to cross the line between what was real and what was pretend?

I could almost feel the kiss before it even happened, the tension hanging in the air so thick it was hard to swallow. And, for a split second, I let myself imagine what it would feel like to have his lips on mine, the world falling away, and everything shifting between us.

But then, right at the edge of that moment, the door to the waiting room swung open, and the sound snapped us both out of it.

Alex walked in.

Of all people.

"Hey," Alex said, glancing between me and Topher like he'd interrupted something.

Which he had.

"Your mom's going to be okay, Mr. Brodie. She was just dehydrated. I'm assisting her doctor, and they asked me to tell you that you can go in."

Topher immediately sat up straighter, his jaw tightening as he fixed his eyes on Alex. There was a sharpness in his expression that I hadn't ever seen before.

"Thanks, Alex," I said quickly, trying to ease the sudden tension in the room.

Alex glanced at me, then back at Topher. "I can stay with Kathleen if you want to go see your mom. I'm on break for another twenty minutes, and the waiting room coffee is terrible. I could grab her something better from the staff lounge."

The temperature in the room seemed to drop ten degrees.

Topher's hand was still in mine, but suddenly his grip tightened —firm, possessive, almost territorial. His thumb had stopped its reassuring circles. Alex had never held my hand like this, like he was afraid to let go, afraid that if he did, I'd slip away, and he couldn't, wouldn't ever let that happen.

Inside, I felt a strange rush of happiness. There was a flutter in my chest, a warmth spreading through me. It was like a quiet reassurance, a feeling of safety, like for once, someone wanted to keep me close. I wanted that too.

"That won't be necessary." Topher's tone was sharp. "She's coming with me."

Alex blinked, clearly caught off guard. "Oh, I just thought—family only, usually—"

"She stays with me," Topher said firmly.

Alex raised his hands in a small gesture of surrender. "Alright, I'll leave you two to it."

He gave me a quick nod before heading out.

As soon as the door clicked shut, I turned to Topher, eyebrows raised. "What was that about?"

Topher's shoulders were still tense, his fists balled at his sides. "I don't trust him," he muttered, his eyes blazing. "I don't like the way he looked at you."

My heart skipped a beat. The intensity in his voice and the hint of possessiveness took me completely by surprise. And the part of me that had secretly been craving Topher's attention couldn't help but like it.

I opened my mouth to respond, but Topher sighed and ran a hand through his hair. "I'm sorry," he said, his voice quieter now. "It's been a long day, and I don't know what came over me."

"It's okay." I kept my tone light even though my heart was racing. "Stress does weird things to people."

Before either of us could say more, the door creaked open again, bringing us back to the present.

"Time to check on your mom," I said softly, nodding toward the hallway.

Topher nodded, his expression softening as we stood and moved toward her room. My pulse quickened, not from the rush of walking but from the memory of that brief moment when I thought he might kiss me.

As we stopped in front of the door, I realized something that made my breath catch. We were still holding hands. We had been holding hands the entire time, and neither of us had let go. His grip was steady, almost like he was afraid to release me, and the truth was, I didn't want him to. I looked at our hands, intertwined, and felt a quiet certainty settle over me. If he didn't seem to want to let go, well then, neither did I.

14

It's funny how quickly you can get used to playing house with a billionaire and his mom. I mean, if you'd asked me a few weeks ago, I would've laughed in your face at the idea of sitting around in a cozy living room, watching *Jeopardy!* with Topher Brodie and his mother.

But there we were.

Josephine was back from the hospital, feeling stronger every day, wrapped in one of her hand-sewn blankets, and leaning back in her chair like a queen on her throne.

Topher sat next to me on the couch, his arm casually slung over my shoulders like it belonged there.

It was all fake, of course. It was just for show.

But I'd noticed something: whenever Topher knew the answer, his arm would tighten around me just before he shouted it out. And then there were his fingers, drawing lazy lines up and down my arm. Was he doing it on purpose? He was so good at pretending, and I was terrible at being the one he pretended with—because the flutter in my chest, the gentle pull low in my stomach, the urge to lean into him and rest my head against his chest? That all felt very real.

The TV droned on in the background, the voice of the game-show host filling the room. Topher, naturally, was dominating. Another question flashed on the screen, something about the structure of DNA, and before I could even blink, Topher said, "What is a double helix?"

I raised an eyebrow. "Okay, Mr. Know-It-All, is there anything you don't know? Like all the numbers of pi?"

Topher grinned, "3.14159—"

"Stop, stop!" I waved my hand, laughing. "I was kidding."

He chuckled. "I could keep going, you know."

Josephine piped up from her chair, "Don't tempt him. He once spent an entire road trip to Pennsylvania telling me every single detail about every NASA mission ever launched."

"Hey, Apollo 11 deserves respect," Topher said, mock offended.

"True, but I don't need to know what everyone on the crew ate for each meal," Josephine joked. "Remember that road trip? We were headed to see some... what was it? That ridiculous science museum?"

Topher grinned. "Ridiculous? Mom, it was the Franklin Institute, and it was incredible. They had an entire exhibit dedicated to the history of space exploration, not to mention the Foucault pendulum. That thing swings for hours without stopping as proof of Earth's rotation."

I stared at him, blinking. "You drove across the country to watch a pendulum swing?"

"Uh, yeah," he said, like it was the most obvious thing in the world. "It's physics in motion. And also, they had a giant heart you could walk through."

Josephine snorted. "Let's just say it was the longest eighteen-hour drive of my life. He kept me entertained by listing all the prime numbers up to one thousand."

Topher grinned. "It's a mental challenge. 2, 3, 5, 7, 11..."

"You're giving me a headache already," I groaned.

Topher grinned down at me. "I'm a delight to go on a road trip with."

Josephine shook her head, eyes twinkling. "You get used to it.

After a while, you just learn to nod along. Or make him take breaks to decorate for Halloween."

"Right, the decorations." I glanced over my shoulder at the window, where our over-the-top haunted beach display was still proudly standing outside. "I think the skeleton lifeguard has officially won over the neighbors."

Topher smirked. "Yeah, he's been pulling in the crowds."

But it wasn't solely the holiday decorations that brought the constant stream of neighbors to the house. It was Josephine. Everyone wanted to hug her or make sure she was okay. People stopped by daily, dropping off gumbo, crawfish pies, and enough jambalaya to feed a small nation.

And she sent each neighbor off with a homemade gift, from scarves she knitted, jars of her famous pickles, or pumpkin-shaped soaps she whipped up in her kitchen. It seemed like everything in her house had her personal touch. The cozy throw blankets on the couch? She'd sewn those herself. The lavender-scented candles on the table? Yep, made by Josephine.

Everyone loved Josephine. How could I not?

And then there was Topher. He had this endearing way of being utterly ridiculous without even realizing it. Take movie nights, for example. It was never just 'watching a movie' with him. We'd sit down with Josephine for a lighthearted comedy, something simple to unwind to. But five minutes in, Topher would be deep into an analysis about how the director completely botched a prime opportunity to play with shadows to enhance the emotional depth. "This scene is *begging* for a chiaroscuro effect," he'd say, munching popcorn like it was the most normal observation in the world.

Then, of course, he'd follow it up with, "And why is that character holding a coffee cup like *that*? Nobody drinks coffee like that unless they're hiding something! He's the culprit!"

The more time we spent together, the more I found myself charmed by his quirks.

I tried really hard not to fall for the cozy family moments, the neighbors treating us like a unit. But with every oddball thing he did, every glance he shot my way, the harder it was to remind myself this was all just pretend. The lines between what was real and what wasn't were starting to blur, and I was finding it difficult to keep my feelings in check.

Just then, the host started reading a brain-busting clue, and before he finished, Topher rattled off the answer. "What is the Treaty of Westphalia?"

Josephine rolled her eyes, shaking her head. "Honestly, who even knows that?"

Topher shrugged. "Uh, anyone who's taken a college course in Advanced Diplomatic Relations of the 17th Century."

I burst out laughing. "Oh, yeah, because that's totally on everyone's bucket list of classes."

Topher looked at me, dead serious. "It should be. I mean, who *wouldn't* want to learn about treaties that literally shaped the modern state system?"

I cut him off, grinning. "Stop. Just stop. You're like a walking Wikipedia page, and it's *infuriating*."

He grinned, grabbing another handful of popcorn. "I prefer 'highly knowledgeable and incredibly humble.'" He flashed me that crooked grin that made my stomach flip.

"Debatable," I shot back.

He chuckled, pulling me closer with a quick, playful tug. Butterflies took flight in my chest. As *Jeopardy!* droned on in the background, I found myself relaxing into him: his warmth, the steady hush of his breathing.

After the next question, I glanced up at him from the crook of his arm. He was thinking, eyes narrowed in concentration, his face so close I could see the subtle shift in his expression as the answer dawned on him.

Then his eyes flicked down to me, softening, and for a split second, I swore he was going to kiss me. My heart pounded in my chest, and I held my breath, waiting.

"Oh, don't let me interrupt," Josephine's voice cut through the moment, laced with amusement. "You two lovebirds carry on."

I blushed and opened my mouth to stammer out a response, but before I could, Topher's lips brushed against mine. It was barely more than a whisper of contact. Yet it sent electricity coursing through my veins.

As he pulled back, a ghost of a smile played at the corners of his mouth. "Happy now, Mom?" he quipped, but his eyes never left mine.

The kiss was barely a brush of his lips, a fleeting touch, but it sent a shockwave through me that I couldn't control. It wasn't the kind of kiss that made your heart race. No, this was something deeper, something that stirred everything inside me, down to the parts I'd kept hidden. His gaze held mine, and it felt like he could see into the darkest corners of my soul. Like he *wanted* to devour whatever he found there.

It had been the lightest kiss, almost not there at all, but it rocked me like an earthquake, like no other kiss had. It obliterated every kiss before it.

My high school boyfriend? Gone. That guy in college? Never happened. Alex? Who? There was only Topher now.

The rush of feelings left me dizzy, as if I'd finally found what I'd been searching for, and now had everything to lose.

Oh no. This wasn't good. I didn't need anyone. I didn't need *this*.

I yawned in a way that I hoped was convincing and stood up quickly. "I'm pretty tired. I think I'll head to bed."

I made my way out of the room, trying to ignore my pounding heart.

But of course, Topher followed, his footsteps trailing behind as I reached the hallway. "Kathleen," he called softly.

I stopped, closing my eyes for a moment before facing him. He was standing so close I could touch him, concern etched on his face.

"What's going on?" His voice was gentle. "You're going to miss Final Jeopardy."

"I'm just exhausted. I think I'll go to bed."

Topher raised an eyebrow, clearly not convinced, but he didn't push. "Alright. I'll go to bed, too."

"It's not even that late," I said, a little louder than necessary, hoping to sound nonchalant. "You should go back and hang out with your mom."

Before he could respond, Josephine's voice floated in from the living room. "No, no, you two go be together. I'm going to bed! And don't worry about me. I've got earplugs and a white noise machine."

My face heated, and I could feel the blush creeping across my cheeks. *If only she knew this was all fake.*

Topher gave a slight shrug, as if to say, '*Well, guess we have no choice.*' I forced a smile, my heart racing, and nodded as we headed into the bedroom.

An awkward silence hung between us. I busied myself with straightening the pillows. Out of the corner of my eye, I noticed Topher watching me.

His eyes lit up, as if he'd just remembered something important. "I looked up a program you might be interested in. Tulane has a social work degree. It's impressive, and with a fellowship, you wouldn't have to worry about the tuition because it would be completely covered."

His words caught me off guard. Topher had been thinking about my future when I hadn't even allowed myself to imagine what might come next.

Something shifted inside me. Topher, who was so often consumed by work, had made space in his mind for me. For my future. He cared enough to imagine possibilities for me.

My heart was full. Josephine had done the same thing, welcoming me into her life without hesitation and treating me like family even though she had just met me. Every little smile she sent my way all added up to a feeling I hadn't had in a long time. The feeling of home. It was all so unexpected. Being here with them made me realize how much I had missed that sense of belonging and being cared for. The way Topher looked at me, the way Josephine made me feel safe. They were showing me what home could look like. What family could be. And for the first time, I allowed myself to want it.

It made me think of my parents, and the ache of missing them tightened around my chest like a weight, making it hard to breathe, but instead of retreating from the emotion, I let it wash over me.

Topher was still talking, outlining the benefits and opportunities of the Tulane program, but his voice faded into the background, muffled by the rush of blood in my ears. I forced a smile, nodding along, while inside, the walls I had meticulously built around my heart began to tremble, threatening to come crashing down.

I didn't need anyone. That was the mantra I'd lived by for years. I was perfectly capable of handling my own problems and messes.

But something about the way Topher looked at me now, with that quiet, patient concern, made it hard to keep those walls up.

He took a step closer, his voice soft. "You seem off. You sure everything's okay?"

A tightness settled in my chest. How did he manage to get past the walls I put up? He was far too perceptive. He sat down on the bed, silently waiting for me to speak.

"What's wrong?" he asked, his voice gentle. I bit my lip, trying to keep the words at bay, but his gaze was so steady, so darn sincere. "You can tell me. It's okay."

It's okay. I wasn't sure how he made those words carry so much weight, but somehow, they did. In that moment, all the stories I'd spun about being self-sufficient, about not needing anyone else, scattered.

I glanced at him, and he gave me the slightest nod. Taking a shaky breath, I sat down on the bed, facing him, and felt a strange sensation rising in my chest, something I hadn't felt in a long time, like it was okay to be vulnerable.

"My parents," I began, the words coming out in a whisper. "They were in so much debt. And they never told me. I had no idea until... until they died."

The room felt heavy with the weight of that confession, but he didn't look away, didn't flinch. His attention was entirely on me as if I were the most important thing in the world. "It was a car accident when I was in my junior year of college." My voice trembled. "After they were gone, I found out how bad things were. They'd kept it all from me, probably trying to protect me, but all it did was leave me with a big mess to clean up. I had to drop out of school, take up dead-end jobs to pay off what they left behind."

Topher reached over, gently enclosing my hand in his. The warmth of his touch sent a jolt through me.

Maybe because Topher made me feel so safe, I confessed the one thing that haunted me the most—the thing that gnawed at me relentlessly, leaving me raw and exposed. "I was such a workaholic in college." The words tumbled out, finally free for the first time. "I stayed in the dorms every break, thought I was being so responsible, so focused on my future. I never went home. I thought I was doing the right thing, but there were so many things I missed."

Topher kept his gaze on me, his thumb brushing lightly over the back of my hand, grounding me in the moment.

"I should have—" I felt the sting of tears in my eyes. "I should have been there for them. I'll never get that time back."

"You did the best you could." His voice was steady. "You were trying to make a future for yourself. You thought you had more time."

A small sob escaped, and I leaned into him. He wrapped his arms around me, and even though there was no one there to see us, he pulled me close.

For the first time in years, I let myself lean on someone else and let someone else take some of the weight.

"This loan company is truly evil," I said. "They won't let me pay the money back early, and the interest rate just keeps climbing. It's like being caught in an endless cycle, constantly spiraling but never actually clearing the debt."

Topher paused, clearly thinking it over. "That sounds incredibly tough. When did they mention the prepayment penalty? Was that upfront, or did they add that in later?"

I raised an eyebrow, smirking slightly. "Uhh, *prepayment penalty?* Fancy." Then, I let out a frustrated huff. "In the fine print, of course. They make it seem normal, and then, bam, you're trapped."

"Do you know if this company is based locally or on one of the coasts?" he asked, his tone careful.

"I don't even know." I shot him a curious look. "Why? Does it matter?"

He coughed. "No, just curious. I'm so sorry this is happening to you."

I nodded, a heavy weight lifting off my chest. It felt oddly freeing to have said it out loud, to have shared this burden with someone else.

In the quiet of the room, wrapped in Topher's embrace, the burdens I'd been carrying for so long started to lift.

It wasn't just that I was being held. It was that *he* was the one holding me. And somehow, that made all the difference.

15

THERE I WAS, sitting across from Luke Fisher.

Yep, *that* Luke Fisher.

Academy Award-winning, People's Sexiest Man Alive, star of every movie that's ever made anyone laugh, cry, and/or question their life choices.

Oh, and apparently, he was Topher's best friend. They had gone to college together and knew each other before they became famous.

And there we all were, crammed into Josephine's tiny house, Luke looking every bit like he was born to lounge on Italian leather, while his wife Anna, who grew up not far from me in New Orleans, looked effortlessly stunning on a thrifted chair that squeaked whenever she moved.

And the weirdest part? I was having fun.

"I knew this guy when he was a full-on nerd," Luke said. "The biggest nerd."

Topher rolled his eyes, but there was a smirk creeping up. "Says the guy who once wrote a ten-page essay on why Spider-Man could outwit Hamlet. And read the whole thing in class. Dressed as Spider-Man."

Luke shrugged, grinning. "It's called *committing* to the role. Maybe that's why I have an Oscar and you have spreadsheets."

Topher leaned back, crossing his arms with a smirk. "At least I wasn't quoting *Twilight* at parties."

Luke gasped dramatically, clutching his chest. "Excuse me? I was Team Jacob for *literary* reasons."

Nerds? These two, looking like they walked off the cover of GQ, had been nerds? I blinked, trying to reconcile the word with the evidence in front of me.

Luke Fisher was tall and tan, with perfectly tousled blonde hair that belonged in a shampoo commercial. He looked like someone you could admire from a distance but never touch. He was effortless, movie-star handsome.

When I first met Topher, I thought he was the same—too perfect, too polished. Tall, with brown hair that always seemed to fall just right, and a jawline so sharp it could cut glass. He wore an intense look, like he was always three steps ahead of everyone else, and honestly? I had figured he'd be just as untouchable as Luke.

But now? The more time I spent with him, the more real he seemed. His eyes weren't so guarded, and when he smiled, it lit up his whole face in a way that made him even more handsome. Less perfect, but better.

Honestly, if this were the new definition of 'nerd,' then sign me up. Where do I get my membership card?

Josephine, who had been quietly watching the college friends joke around, finally chimed in. "I'm just glad to see that time hasn't changed either of you."

Anna turned to Josephine with a warm smile, smoothly shifting the conversation. "We're just so glad you're feeling better. You look amazing."

Josephine smiled, waving her hand dismissively. "Oh, please. It's all the lounging around I've been doing. I haven't even had your spa people come yet. Thank you for that gift, by the way."

Anna reached over and touched her arm. "You deserve to be pampered!"

Josephine chuckled. "I know, I know! It's just, well, with Topher and his *darling* Kathleen staying here, I've been so spoiled already."

Luke raised an eyebrow. "Toph? *Spoiling* someone? Did I wake up in an alternate universe?"

Josephine patted Luke's hand and lowered her voice. "I know. For years, I saw you more than I saw Topher because he would never come home. But now he's here, and he and Kathleen are making my meals. Can you believe it?"

Her words struck me. Why would she have seen Luke more than her own son? That seemed odd. But no one else in the room even blinked, as if this was just a well-known fact about Topher, that he was always so focused on work that his family slipped into the background.

Before I could unpack it any further, Luke turned to me, eyes wide. "Topher? In the kitchen? *Voluntarily?* Are we sure he's not just boiling water and calling it a meal?"

I laughed. "Believe it. Topher's an impressive chef. He's been whisking together some gourmet dishes."

Josephine added with a smile, "And our favorite part of the day is watching *Jeopardy!* together and then a movie to unwind. We even saw one of yours the other night—*The Last Stand*."

Anna's grin widened as she rubbed Luke's knee affectionately. "*The Last Stand*? The one where Luke was the retired soldier who swore he'd never fight again. Until the bad guys show up and— surprise—he fights again?"

Josephine nodded enthusiastically. "I was gripping my chair during that final battle. I'm pretty sure I forgot to breathe."

"Yeah, I had to remind *myself* to breathe filming that scene." Luke mimed dragging something heavy. "Turns out, carrying a life-size dummy of my co-star was more of a workout than I signed up for."

"You know," Anna said, smiling, "I always thought you'd move on to something calmer after that, but nope, you went straight to another action movie."

Luke grinned. "I do love a good explosion. Keeps the audience awake."

Josephine chuckled. "Well, we appreciated the adrenaline rush. It's not every day you get to watch someone you know save the world."

"And he only had to blow up half a city to do it," Topher added, deadpan.

Luke shot him a mischievous grin. "I can't believe it. Topher Brodie watching movies. Playing *Jeopardy!*? Making meals and not glued to his work? This *is* an alternate reality."

Josephine's eyes twinkled. "And these two are responsible for all those Halloween decorations outside. Can you believe it?"

Anna's jaw dropped, and she turned to us. "Wait, *you two* did that? Topher, arranging holiday decorations? Now I've heard everything."

Topher raised his coffee mug in a mock toast. "Well, to be fair, my assistant did most of the heavy lifting. But we provided, uh, *creative direction.*"

I couldn't help but laugh. "It was all Topher. My 'creative direction' mostly consisted of pointing and saying, 'more pumpkins.'"

Topher grinned, his eyes twinkling with mischief. "Yeah, the real highlight was Kathleen's battle with a spider web. It was legendary."

I groaned. "Don't even start."

"Oh, I *have* to." He leaned in, mock serious. "She walked into it and somehow, in under five seconds, managed to look like a Halloween mummy."

I rolled my eyes but couldn't help laughing. "You weren't much help. You stood there for a good minute, saying, 'I'm pretty sure it's not *real*, Kathleen,' while I was fighting for my life."

Topher chuckled. "Hey, I was offering moral support."

I shot him a playful glare. "Oh, right. You just stood there like a director yelling, *More drama! Make it more believable!*"

We burst into laughter, lost in the memory, and when I finally looked up, Anna and Luke were staring at us wide-eyed.

I cleared my throat. "I guess you had to be there."

Luke shook his head. "First meal prep, now holiday decor. Next thing we know, Topher'll be baking pies from scratch."

"Don't get ahead of yourself," Topher said. "One miracle at a time."

We laughed, and as the evening wore on, Josephine stood up, stretching with a satisfied sigh. She gave Luke and Anna warm hugs. "You kids behave now. I'm off to bed. Don't stay up too late reliving the glory days."

"No promises," Topher said.

As Josephine left, the guys naturally veered into what was apparently one of their favorite topics: their rowing days at Brown, when they were both athletes *and* masochists.

"Do you remember that one race where we were so wiped afterward, we had to crawl to the showers?" Topher said with a grin.

Luke laughed. "Right! The only thing that saved my grades that semester was the fact that I physically couldn't fall asleep in class because my muscles were too sore to relax."

Topher chuckled. "And remember that one guy on the team who rowed until his hands bled? That guy was a *legend*."

Luke gave him a look. "Yeah, I remember. That guy was you."

Topher smirked. "Well, someone had to show the rest of you what commitment looked like."

Luke shook his head. "Or what insanity looked like."

Topher laughed. "Speaking of insanity, remember that time I rowed so hard I threw up mid-stroke and kept going? There was no way I was letting my team down."

"Ha! That's nothing. Don't you remember when I puked so hard it splashed into the opponent's boat during a sprint? They were so freaked out that we won the race. Now *that's* legendary."

Anna wrinkled her nose. "Okay, when these guys start talking about vomiting, that's my cue to cut out." She turned to me with a smile. "Want to get some air?"

The cool evening breeze hit my skin as we stepped onto the porch. I glanced over at Anna, marveling for a moment at how effort- lessly stunning she was. Her waves of brown hair glinted in the light. She looked like she should be on the cover of some glossy magazine, yet she was so easy-going, the kind of woman you could share a pizza with while binge-watching terrible TV. Not at all like the wife of a movie star. Way cooler, actually.

"How are you doing?" Anna's voice was gentle, but with a hint of curiosity.

"I'm fine. Just glad Josephine's doing so much better."

Anna smiled slightly, tilting her head as if she knew something I didn't. "You don't have to pretend with me."

I raised an eyebrow. "Pretend?"

"I know the whole romance between you and Topher isn't real."

My heart skipped a beat. Was it that obvious?

"Topher told Luke," she explained. "Those two can't keep anything from each other." Then Anna leaned in just a bit, as if she wanted to share a secret. "Topher might be saying that it's fake, but I've never seen him act like this before."

I tried to laugh it off and shook my head. Sure, Topher had done thoughtful things—like bringing me my favorite coffee and remem- bering little details I'd casually mentioned. But wasn't that just part of keeping up the act? He was playing his role perfectly, just like I was. Right?

And then there was the way he'd started talking about my future. Social work school, putting together a plan for me. But that wasn't love. It was logistics. He was simply ensuring things went smoothly when this charade came to an end, tying up loose ends.

But Anna's next words made my heart flutter with something I hadn't been ready to feel. "You may not see it, but I do. He's letting his guard down with you in a way he hasn't with anyone else."

Could Anna be right? Could all those small, seemingly insignificant moments add up to something more? My heart thumped, the excitement bubbling up inside me before I could even process it. I hadn't let myself hope that this could be anything beyond an act, a charade to help his mother feel better. But now, standing here with Anna's words hanging in the air, I started to wonder. Had he been dropping hints all along?

Just as the thought began to take shape, the door creaked open, and Topher stepped outside, Luke following behind him. They were mid-conversation, but Topher's eyes found mine instantly. And there it was—that look. The one I hadn't allowed myself to read into before, the one that felt soft and focused, like he saw something in me that no one else did.

My pulse quickened, and every word Anna had just said echoed in my mind.

"Kathleen," Topher said, his voice calm but carrying a warmth I hadn't expected, "I was just telling Luke about the social work program at Tulane. How perfect I think you'd be for it."

I blinked, completely thrown. He had been talking about me? Even when I wasn't around? The idea sent my thoughts into a spiral, something electric unfurled in my chest.

Suddenly, everything Anna had said hit me all at once. The soft glances, the thoughtful gestures, the way he always seemed to want to make sure I was okay. It wasn't just about fooling his mom or keeping up appearances. Topher's feelings weren't just part of the act. They were real. And the more I thought about it, the more undeniable it became.

The excitement built inside me, my mind spinning with possibilities I hadn't allowed myself to imagine before. And now that I was starting to see it, I couldn't unsee it.

I couldn't stop smiling, my heart swelling with a hope that had been buried for far too long.

For the first time in a long time, I let myself believe in the possibility of something good. And it felt amazing.

"Alright," Anna said, glancing at her phone. "We should probably get going. Early flight tomorrow."

Luke nodded. "The pilots are sticklers for takeoff times, even with a private plane. They like to keep things running smoothly."

Anna rolled her eyes, linking her arm with his. "Yeah, smoothly until we're sitting on the tarmac because someone forgot something important *again*."

"Hey," Luke replied, a hint of a smile on his lips, "one time I forgot my passport. One. Time. And I told you, it wasn't even that important."

Topher grinned, shaking his head. "Not that important, huh? You might want to rethink that strategy if you plan on ever leaving the country again."

Luke gave him a playful shove. "That's what private planes are for, my friend. They let you get away with that stuff. But I *guess* we should get there on time, just to be nice."

"Generous of you," Topher teased. "Don't want to upset the pilot. Wouldn't want him holding up takeoff because of, you know, *poor planning*."

Luke groaned dramatically. "Man, you hold onto one little thing..."

"Little thing?" Topher laughed. "Forgetting your passport is huge, Luke. I'm surprised Anna even lets you pack your own bags."

Anna smiled knowingly. "Oh, he doesn't. That's why we're always on time now."

Luke shrugged, conceding with a grin, then looked at her like she was the best thing that had ever happened to him. "Hey, at least I've got you to keep me in line."

When they were getting ready to leave, Anna hugged me as Luke turned to Topher. "Take care, Kathleen," she whispered. "And take care of him too," she added with a soft wink.

"I will," I promised, squeezing her before she stepped back.

Luke and Anna slipped into the back of the car, the door clicking shut behind them. Their driver started the engine, and the headlights illuminated the driveway. Topher and I stood on the porch, side by side, waving as the car rolled away, disappearing down the road.

For a moment, the quiet settled in around us, and I felt a peaceful kind of warmth. I smiled, then turned toward the door, ready to head inside. But before I could even reach for the handle, I felt Topher's hand grab mine, stopping me in my tracks. His grip was firm but gentle, and as I turned back, he didn't let go. Instead, he pulled me back toward him, outside, right into his arms.

My heart thumped so loudly I swore he could hear it. I looked up at him, caught completely off guard. "What... what is this about?" My voice was barely above a whisper.

There was a sweet shyness in the way he looked down at me. He swallowed, his eyes searching mine, and in that moment, he seemed almost vulnerable.

"I want to take you on a date. A real date. No acting, no pretending. Because... what I'm feeling isn't pretend."

I blinked, my breath catching as his words sank in. He was still holding my hand, and I could feel the warmth of it.

"I need to know if this is real." He spoke carefully, sounding almost shy. "I need to find out if I still feel the same when no one's looking." Then he cleared his throat, the hint of doubt appearing to fall away, and when he spoke again, there was a quiet certainty in his tone, like he had made up his mind. "But I'm not particularly worried. No one's looking now, and I feel... everything."

My heart swelled, and for a second, the world tilted on its axis. I could barely process the rush of emotions flooding through me. All I knew was that he was standing here, telling me exactly what I needed to hear.

I opened my mouth to respond, but the words didn't come out right away. Instead, a soft laugh escaped my lips, filled with a mix of surprise and happiness. Inside, my heart was practically screaming, *Yes, yes, yes!* But I forced myself to stay cool. I bit back the smile threatening to give me away and nodded, trying to keep my voice steady.

"I think…" I whispered, my voice catching slightly, "I think I'd really like that."

He smiled, a real, genuine smile that made my heart skip, and I felt a wave of happiness wash over me. "Good, because I've wanted this for a while. I just didn't realize it until now."

A warmth spread through me, and everything clicked. We were on the same page, stepping into something real. And as I looked up at him, I knew that this was just the beginning.

16

In all the possible versions of a first date with Topher Brodie, *this* was not the one I imagined. There was no candlelit rooftop, no private chef, no tasteful jazz trio in the corner. Instead, there was a giant swan boat, two very uncoordinated adults, and a suspiciously judgmental duck watching from the shore.

Topher gripped the oversized handles of the swan boat, his brow furrowed in concentration. "I did not realize that pedaling a giant swan would be this complicated," he said, shooting me a helpless look.

I burst out laughing, my legs struggling to reach the pedals. "We've been pedaling for what feels like forever, and I swear we've barely moved."

Topher groaned, shaking his head. "We've got to be the least coordinated swan boat riders ever."

I couldn't stop laughing; the sheer ridiculousness of the situation made it impossible to take anything seriously. "Hey, I think we've officially lapped that same tree like three times. This is swan boat purgatory."

"You're not wrong," he said, wiping his brow dramatically. "At this rate, we'll be out here until next week."

"You know, I'm kind of impressed with how bad we are at this." I laughed as I tried to steer us back on course.

"You say 'we,' but I think you're doing just fine." Topher nudged me lightly. "I'm the one who keeps steering us straight into the shore."

"I think we've redefined what counts as a romantic date," I teased. "But you know what? I'm having a great time."

Topher shot me a sideways glance, his smile softening. "Yeah? Even with the whole swan boat disaster?"

I nodded, still grinning. "*Especially* with the swan boat disaster. It's the most fun I've had in a while."

He looked at me for a long moment, his expression shifting from playful to something more serious, something I wasn't quite expecting. "I'm glad we're doing this." He took a deep breath, as if he were choosing his words carefully. "Obviously, I didn't think everything through when we got into this whole fake relationship thing. I wasn't sure how it would play out. But it's been different from what I expected. Better, honestly."

My heart fluttered, and the air between us felt charged, like the whole mood had shifted into something deeper. "Better how?" I asked softly, trying to keep my voice steady, even though my pulse was racing.

Topher paused, his hands resting on the swan boat's handles, his gaze softening as he looked at me. "I didn't expect to... like this. To like *you*." He smiled, a bit more tender now, and my breath hitched. "I mean, you're smart and funny, and you challenge me in a way no one else does. You don't just let me get away with stuff—you push me to be better."

I felt my cheeks heat, and for once, I was glad the ridiculous swan boat was distracting enough to hide how flustered I was.

"And you have this way of making people feel comfortable, like they can be themselves. I've seen it with my mom. You've been so good to her, and it's not just an act. It's who you are." He looked down for a second, as if he were gathering his thoughts, then met my gaze again, more earnest this time. "You make me feel like I can be myself around you. Like, I don't have to be 'Topher Brodie' the billionaire or whatever. I'm just... me."

I blinked, his words hitting me right in the chest, and I had to swallow down the lump forming in my throat. I'd always known Topher was more than what people saw on the surface, but hearing him say these things about me, about how I made *him* feel, was almost overwhelming.

He hesitated, his eyes searching mine. "And you've made me realize something else, too. I don't have to keep grinding myself into the ground. You've shown me that it's okay to take a step back. I've been here for weeks now, and I haven't worked as hard as I used to. But you know what? Nothing's fallen apart. My life hasn't collapsed." He let out a small, almost disbelieving laugh. "I'm happier, less stressed, and feeling better than I ever have in my life. And that's because of you."

My heart pounded as his words sank in. Topher Brodie, the workaholic billionaire who never stopped moving, was admitting he didn't want to work as hard. And he was attributing it to *me*.

"Topher," I whispered, my voice trembling slightly. I wanted to say something, but my mind was spinning too fast, trying to keep up with the enormity of what this meant.

He smiled, a little softer now, and reached over and gave my hand a quick, reassuring squeeze—just enough to make my heart trip over itself. "I don't want to go back to the way things were before. You've made me realize there's more to life than working nonstop. I want more than that."

I swallowed hard, my heart swelling. "That's, that's a big step for you. I mean, you've been on this path for so long, and now you're saying—"

"I'm saying I'm willing to change," he interrupted, his tone sincere. "For me. And maybe for us."

I couldn't help it. The joy that bubbled up inside me was impossible to hide. My lips curved into a wide, uncontrollable smile. "Wow, that's... that's huge."

He grinned, and his eyes never left mine. "Yeah, well... you're kind of a big deal." His voice softened even more. "You pay attention to the little things. You notice when I'm stressed, even if I try to hide it. You don't miss anything. And I didn't realize how much I needed someone like that in my life."

I stared at him, my heart thumping with every word he spoke. He wasn't just saying nice things—he was *seeing* me, and it felt like the most genuine thing in the world.

"I don't know how to explain it," he said, his voice dropping a little lower. "But when I'm with you, it feels like everything just... fits."

I felt my heart soar, and the smile that spread across my face was impossible to hide. "Topher—" My voice cracked, and I had to laugh at myself. "I don't know what to say."

He grinned, reaching out to brush a strand of hair behind my ear. "I know we started this whole thing for my mom, to make her happy. But it doesn't feel like we're pretending anymore. At least not to me."

I swallowed hard, my mind racing as I tried to process what he was saying. "What are you saying?"

His smile was soft but sincere. "I don't want to just play along anymore. I want us to give this a try."

The world seemed to pause for a second. Well, at least it did in my head. The ridiculous swan boat, the swirling water, all of it faded into the background as his words hung between us. I couldn't stop the warmth that spread through me, and before I could even think twice, the words tumbled out. "I like spending time with you, too."

The second I said it, I realized how true it was. It wasn't planned, but it felt so right, so easy. And the look on his face—his grin stretching wider, relief lighting up his eyes—it only made me happier.

"Good," he said, his voice warm and carrying the same quiet happiness that had started to build in me.

And then, *thud*! Our swan boat jerked violently to the side, slamming into another swan boat with a loud *clunk*. We lurched forward, gripping the handles for dear life as we tried not to tip over.

"Oh no, I think we hit them!" I gasped, my eyes wide with shock, but the sight of the startled couple in the other boat only made me want to laugh. They stared at us, wide-eyed.

"Oops," Topher said with a sheepish grin. "Sorry!"

Nobody had been injured, but the bump sent our perfectly packed picnic basket tumbling off the boat's edge. "No, no, no!" I yelled, watching it fall in slow motion, flipping dramatically into the lagoon with a loud *splash*.

For a moment, we both just stared at the floating basket, bobbing along in the water. Then, all at once, the absurdity of the situation hit, and I doubled over with laughter. "Oh, no, did we just lose our lunch to the lagoon?"

Topher was laughing, too, his hands still gripping the handles. "My mom and Gladys are going to love this story."

"We have to rescue it!" I said, still giggling. "We can't let the sandwiches go down without a fight!"

Topher shook his head, already turning the swan in the general direction of the basket, but it was clear this boat had a mind of its own. Instead of going straight, we veered to the left, circling the basket as if we were predators who couldn't quite figure out how to catch their prey.

"Pedal faster!" I shouted, trying to get us closer.

"I am!" Topher exclaimed, his face red with effort, though he was laughing too hard to be of any real help.

"Weren't you, like, some big rowing star at Brown? Shouldn't you be *killing* this?" I teased, barely keeping a straight face as the swan boat wobbled hopelessly off course.

Topher groaned, trying to steer with no success. "First of all, real rowing doesn't involve giant plastic birds, okay? This is completely different!"

"Sure, keep telling yourself that." We lurched forward, then backward, our coordination as awful as ever, and I could see the basket drifting farther and farther away. "We're losing it! The sandwiches are floating to their doom!"

"Okay, okay, we've got this," Topher said, but his voice shook with laughter. We finally managed to get close enough to the basket, and I leaned over, stretching out my arm to grab it.

"Careful, careful!" Topher warned, half-serious, half-laughing. "We don't need to go down with the ship!"

I was just inches from the basket when—*plop!*—my hand slipped, and I tipped forward. Topher yanked me back into the boat just as I was about to swan dive into the lagoon, his strong arms wrapping around me as I landed ungracefully in his lap. For a second, we just stared at each other, my heart racing for reasons that had nothing to do with the near-drowning incident.

And then he kissed me.

Now, that *Jeopardy!* kiss? The one that had put every kiss from my past to shame? Well, this kiss put that kiss to shame in a way I didn't even know was possible. This kiss was everything I hadn't let myself think about. It was warm, slow, and steady, as if he had all the time in the world and no intention of letting me go anytime soon.

My brain short-circuited. Fireworks? Check. Butterflies? More like a tornado. I felt like I was floating, even though we were technically still stuck in the swan boat. If this is what kissing him was like, how had I not realized sooner that I was completely and utterly gone for him?

"Uh, guys? Your picnic basket is sinking!"

I blinked, dazed, pulling back just slightly to register the words coming from the swan boat we had collided with. I glanced over and, sure enough, there was our sad little picnic basket slowly disappearing beneath the water.

Topher glanced at it, too, and his eyes snapped back to me, his grin playful. "Do you care?"

I shook my head, biting back a smile. "Not even a little."

"Good," he said, pulling me closer again. "Because I've got other things on my mind."

We watched as the basket bobbed one last time before sinking fully out of sight.

"RIP sandwiches," I murmured, not bothering to move.

"Yeah, RIP," Topher echoed, though his focus was back on me.

Honestly? Letting the picnic basket go was the easiest decision I'd ever made. There were more important things happening here.

17

IF YOU'VE NEVER EXPERIENCED emotional whiplash via a hospital-room UNO game, I highly recommend it.

One minute, Topher and I were whispering sweet nothings. The next, we were locked in a full-blown card war, grinning like lunatics and sabotaging each other with the kind of competitive glee that would make Olympic athletes nervous.

I slapped down a Draw Two with a dramatic flourish.

Topher's jaw dropped. "You're heartless."

He drew two cards with a groan, but the gleam in his eyes said otherwise.

"It's UNO," I said, shrugging. "There are no survivors."

Josephine, lounging on the hospital bed like a queen observing court drama, chuckled in approval. With a sly wink, she tossed down a Skip card, shooting the turn right back to me.

What had started as a simple distraction during Josephine's checkup had quickly turned into an all-out battle. But the best part? The way Topher kept finding subtle ways to touch me—his fingers brushing mine when he handed over a card, his leg casually bumping against me as we sat side by side. Each little contact caused a spark, making it impossible to wipe the giddy smile off my face.

I leaned back, still lightheaded from the way Topher's fingers had brushed mine for just a second longer than necessary. "It's not my fault that some of us take competition seriously. It's called *winning*, Topher. Maybe you've heard of it?"

He scoffed. "Oh, I know all about winning. What I didn't realize is that apparently, we can't play *anything* without it becoming a battle for survival."

Josephine laughed. "Remember when we played Pictionary with Gladys? You two spent ten minutes arguing over whether your stick figure was supposed to be a horse or a giraffe."

I crossed my arms. "It was a horse, obviously."

Topher groaned. "A horse? It had horns!"

I shrugged innocently. "That's just artistic flair."

Topher shook his head, drawing his cards. "This is why 'friendly' isn't in our vocabulary."

"You should've known better than to challenge me to anything," I teased, the warmth from his earlier touch still buzzing through me. "Remember the last time we played Monopoly?"

Topher winced dramatically. "Don't remind me. I'm still recovering from losing Park Place." He held up his single card with a smirk. "UNO!"

I quickly threw down a yellow three, but not before our hands brushed against each other again. This time, Topher's fingers lingered, curling around mine like it was the most natural thing in the world. My heart stuttered in my chest, and a giddy rush spread through me. Every touch, every stolen glance, made it harder to focus on the game. I squeezed his hand back, barely able to keep the grin off my face.

I tried to keep my eyes on the game, but the warmth of his hand made it impossible to focus. Curiosity got the better of me, and I glanced at him, only to find his eyes already on me. His gaze was steady, and the soft, heartwarming smile that tugged at his lips sent a rush of heat through me, making my pulse race all over again.

Josephine's eyes flickered to our joined hands, and she smiled knowingly. "You know, I'm happy both of you came with me to the doctor today." Her voice was soft, almost tender. "It means a lot to have you here."

I felt another slight tug in my chest, her words pulling at something deeper. The moment felt sweet, almost like we were a little team.

Then, with a glint in her eye, Josephine's tone shifted to one of pure mischief. She slapped down a Draw Four card with the precision of someone who had planned this moment all along, her grin wide as Topher groaned.

"Ruthless," he muttered.

Josephine grinned proudly. "And don't you forget it."

The room filled with laughter, but all I could focus on was the warmth of Topher's hand still in mine and the way each little touch made me feel like I was floating.

I was ready to throw another teasing jab when the door creaked open, cutting through the moment.

Alex stepped inside, his expression serious as his eyes landed on our intertwined hands. Something shifted in his face, a quick flicker of surprise, before he masked it. "Dr. Julius wants to speak with you, Mrs. Brodie. Nothing urgent, just some health updates. But immediate family only."

As I stood up and walked to follow Alex to the door, Topher shifted in his seat, his eyes meeting mine. He looked uneasy, his brow furrowed. His fingers twitched slightly, like he wanted to say something.

Without thinking, I smiled softly and reached out, my hand brushing gently against his shoulder. "I'll be right back."

He nodded, and the tension in his eyes eased.

I left with Alex, his overly crisp shirt and tousled brown hair doing nothing to stir the emotions they once had. I could objectively admit that Alex was still ridiculously good-looking, but in a "Ken doll who models for budget cologne ads" kind of way. His shirt was so crisp that it looked as if it had just been steamed, and his hair was perfectly styled, with what I knew was an entire shelf of hair products.

"How are you?" Alex asked, his voice softer than I expected, like he was actually interested in the answer for once.

I raised an eyebrow, half expecting a catch. "I'm really good. I've been considering returning to school for a career in social work. I might want to be a therapist."

Alex blinked, clearly taken aback. "A therapist? Really?"

"Yeah." I nodded, surprising even myself with how sure I sounded. "I think I'd be good at it."

To my surprise, a small smile tugged at the corners of his mouth. "You would be. You've always had a way of helping people, getting them to open up."

I grinned, feeling a wave of genuine happiness wash over me. How did this happen? Life was good, and I was right where I was supposed to be. Almost four weeks ago, I'd been fired, evicted, and dumped in one spectacularly bad string of events. Now, there I was, feeling on top of the world. It was almost ridiculous. Who would've guessed I'd be smiling at my ex, feeling generous enough even to humor this conversation?

"Thanks," I said, the absurdity of it all settling in. "Things have been really... falling into place."

His eyes roamed over my face like he was searching for something. "You look so good. Really. You've got this glow about you."

I looked terrific, and I knew it. I couldn't stop smiling. I'd slipped into a simple, fitted dress that hugged my curves in all the right places, and my hair was having one of those rare, glorious days where it fell in soft waves as if I'd just stepped out of a shampoo commercial. For once, Alex's polished, over-the-top appearance didn't rattle me. I felt fantastic, and it showed.

"And now, you've got a plan, and you're moving forward." Alex paused briefly before adding, "Oh, and by the way, things didn't work out with Dr. Sparks. It turns out that two doctors shouldn't be together. You can only handle so much medical talk at home. We'd argue over the best way to set a broken toe or the most effective antihistamine for a mild allergic reaction. One time, we even had a full-blown debate over the pros and cons of different types of surgical sutures... over dinner. Honestly, it was exhausting. So yeah, that fizzled out."

Yes, things were on an upward trajectory for me, but I couldn't help feeling a flicker of satisfaction. "Really? It sounded like a match made in heaven." My tone was laced with sarcasm, but Alex didn't take the bait.

He took a small step closer, his gaze lingering on me as if he couldn't quite believe what he was seeing. "Honestly, I can't stop thinking about you. You're even more amazing than before." Alex shook his head, running a hand through his hair. "I'm sorry, okay? I never should've walked away from you."

I let out a shocked laugh, the kind that comes when someone says something so outrageous you can't believe it's real. "Walked away? You didn't *walk away*. You cheated on me."

He winced but stepped closer. "I want a do-over."

"There's no 'do-over' for what you did."

His expression darkened with frustration. "I get it now. You think this guy cares about you, don't you?"

I clenched my jaw, every muscle in my body tensing. Before I could respond, Alex kept going, his voice dripping with arrogance. "You can't seriously believe that a billionaire who's dated the world's most beautiful women would choose you. Tell me you're not that naïve. He's *Topher Brodie*. He's got women throwing themselves at him. How could he possibly be interested in *you*?"

My pulse quickened, and I felt the edges of my smile slip away. The warmth of Topher's touch, his sweet words, still lingered in the back of my mind, but Alex's words were getting louder, trying to drown out my happiness. I swallowed hard, willing myself not to lose that feeling just because of Alex's bitterness.

"Why does it even matter to you?" I snapped, my voice sharper than I intended.

He stepped closer, his eyes scanning me like he had some right to. "I mean, look at you. You're more gorgeous than ever, and you've got your life together. You're motivated and driven. Everything I always wanted."

A bitter laugh escaped before I could stop it, the memory burning more than I cared to admit. "You dumped me right after I lost my job."

"That was a mistake!" He sounded almost indignant, as if I were the one being unreasonable. "You weren't what I wanted then, but you are now."

I stared at him, incredulous. "Are you even hearing yourself? You think you can just show up and say, 'Oops, my bad,' and everything will be fine? You cheated on me!"

Alex grimaced, as if he were tired of this conversation. "When are you going to stop fixating on that?"

"Never, Alex. Never."

He grabbed my arm lightly, his expression softening, as if he was trying to make me understand. "Come on, I'm serious. I want us to try again."

I yanked my arm back, staring him down. "You want to get back together because I look better now? Because I've 'changed'? News-flash. *You* haven't. You're still the same guy who tore me down when I was at my lowest."

"Do you really think someone like Topher Brodie, whose life is private planes, mansions, and yachts, is going to stay with you? Your life is dropping out of college and driving an airport shuttle. No, wait, *getting fired* from driving an airport shuttle."

I stood my ground, trying not to let him get under my skin. "Regardless of what you think, I'd never get back together with you.

You lied, you cheated, and you made me feel like I was never enough. I'm not going to settle for that again."

I bit out the words, willing myself to stay calm, even though his words cut deeper than I wanted to admit.

Alex scoffed. "Face it. You're not built for a serious relationship. There's just some fundamental part of you that's missing. I always felt like I was dating a stranger. You shut me out of anything real, anything that mattered." He crossed his arms, his gaze cold. "And, you know what? Topher's not going to stick around for that."

The words hit me like a punch to the gut, my fists clenching as I fought to hold my ground. A small, unwelcome thought wormed its way into my mind: *What if he's right? What if I'm not built for a serious relationship?* I'd always held people at a safe distance, built walls that even I didn't know how to break down.

But I forced myself to stand taller, to keep my voice steady. "Just because you couldn't handle me doesn't mean no one can."

Alex laughed, a hollow sound that felt designed to sting. "Keep telling yourself that. But people get tired, Kathleen. They get tired of trying to get through those walls you put up. Brodie might be playing along now, but when he sees the real you? He'll be gone."

I swallowed, the doubt clawing at me despite my best efforts. *Could he be right? Would Topher see the parts of me I kept hidden and decide it wasn't worth it?*

But I wasn't about to let Alex see that he'd rattled me. "Maybe the problem wasn't me, Alex. Maybe it was that you never gave me a reason to trust you."

His smirk faltered, just for a second, before he plastered it back on. "Believe whatever helps you sleep at night, Kathleen. But when he leaves—and he will—don't say I didn't warn you."

I watched him walk away. Leave it to Alex to stir up doubt when things were finally starting to feel good. Liking Topher was risky. I knew that. Letting myself fall for him felt like stepping into the unknown, like jumping off a cliff and hoping I landed safely. It was thrilling, but there was no denying the uncertainty creeping in.

Just as I was trying to shake the thought, my phone buzzed in my pocket. I pulled it out, freezing when I saw the number. The loan company.

I hesitated, then answered, trying to steady my voice. "Hello?"

"This is Amy from Pinnacle Loan Company. Is this Kathleen Avery?"

"Y-yes."

"Good afternoon, Ms. Avery. I'm calling today because you haven't responded to the email we sent you on October twentieth," came the flat, emotionless voice on the other end. "Your payment is overdue. If you don't make the next payment soon, we'll have to double the interest rate. And if it goes to court, you'll be responsible for all legal fees."

My throat tightened. "I... I'm working on it. I'll have the money soon. Please don't increase the rate. I can't afford that. I'll never be able to pay it back."

"You've already had more time than we typically allow," the voice droned on, like they were reading from a script. "You need to make the payment, or we'll proceed with the next steps."

"I'll figure it out," I whispered, but even as I said it, I felt like I was sinking deeper. The weight of the debt pressed down on me, and no matter how much I tried to swim toward the surface, I couldn't break free. I should've been looking for a job this whole time instead of playing house with Topher and Josephine. Now, I'd never be able to clear this loan.

My hand shook as I hung up the phone, the desperation clawing at me. For a split second, I was tempted to ask Topher for help. He could probably make this payment without even thinking twice. All it would take was a word, and the problem could disappear.

But then Alex's words echoed in my head. *How could he possibly be interested in you? You're not built for a serious relationship.*

What if Alex was right? What if Topher wasn't someone I could truly rely on? Sure, he might give me the money, but that didn't mean he cared. I'd be another task on his endless to-do list, another problem to solve and move on from. And the thought of opening up to someone, only to be left behind, made me hesitate.

Or what if he realized I wasn't good enough for him? A billionaire couldn't be with a debt-riddled college dropout. He'd see that for sure if I asked for money.

No, I would figure this out on my own. I wasn't about to lean on someone else. Depending on other people had never worked out for me before. Why would this time be any different?

I was still trying to make sense of it all when I saw Topher down the hall. His face lit up when he spotted me.

He jogged over. "Hey," he said, breathless, a smile in his eyes. "Mom's doing great. She's just wrapping up with the physical therapist now."

"That's good," I replied, keeping my tone even, as my mind spun out of control. Alex's words stuck with me, poisoning everything. Topher glanced over at me, his brow furrowing slightly. "You okay? You seem a little distracted."

I shrugged, trying to shake off the heavy thoughts. "Just a long day."

He didn't let it drop, though. Instead, he leaned closer, his arm brushing mine. The warmth of his touch sent a flicker of heat through me, even as my mind tried to pull me in the opposite direction. He pointed at a sign on the wall. "*Please Do Not Remove the Lobby Plants*? Really?"

I smiled, grateful for the distraction. "People are stealing fake plants now?"

Topher laughed, his voice warm. "I'd love to see someone just casually walking out of here with a giant plastic fern under their arm."

I grinned. "Walk confidently enough, and no one will question it. 'Excuse me, sir, is that hospital property?' 'No, it's my emotional support fern.'"

Topher lost it, his laughter loud and genuine. Seeing him like that, laughing with abandon, made me feel warm inside.

But as the laughter faded, he glanced at me, and his smile softened. His hand rested on mine. His fingers brushed against my skin, his thumb tracing slow circles on the back of my hand.

"When you went off with Alex earlier..." His voice was quieter now, his gaze locked on mine.

My heart quickened. "What about it?"

He hesitated for another moment, then sighed softly. "I didn't like it. Seeing you with him."

My heart stuttered. His hand, still on mine, pressed just a little harder, his thumb still moving in those small, deliberate circles. For a brief moment, the warmth of his touch and the sincerity in his eyes made me want to believe him. Made me want to sink into that feeling and forget everything else.

But then, Alex's voice echoed in my mind: *You're not built for a serious relationship. There's just some fundamental part of you that's missing.* Alex knew the truth: I wasn't amazing at all.

Topher's hand stayed on mine, the pressure increasing slightly, and his eyes searched mine, hopeful, like he was opening a door between us, inviting me to step through. But instead of letting him in, I gently withdrew my hand.

His gaze flickered with a brief flash of hurt, but it disappeared so quickly I wondered if I imagined it.

Then, Josephine walked into the room with her usual bright smile, her presence immediately shifting the energy. Topher straightened, stepping toward his mom, his attention now entirely on her.

"Ready to head home?" Josephine asked, glancing between us with a tired but warm smile.

Once we arrived back at the house, Topher turned to me with a cautious look, almost as if he was afraid of what he might hear but needed to ask anyway.

"You seemed a little distant at the hospital," he said, searching my face. "Is everything okay?"

I swallowed, knowing I owed him honesty, even if it wasn't easy to say.

"It's this, Topher. It's us," I began, feeling the weight of each word. "I have so much to worry about right now. I'm not sure I have time for a relationship. When it was fake... There was no pressure. But now..." I sighed, feeling myself retreat as I said it. "I'm sorry, Topher. I have to focus on finding a job and... and figuring out how to pay my loan."

His hand twitched slightly, like he was about to reach out. "I can—"

"No," I interrupted, shaking my head. "You can't. I can't count on anyone else to fix things for me. I need to do this on my own."

He held my gaze for a moment, as if he were considering saying something more. Then, almost imperceptibly, he nodded, his expression unreadable. He turned and walked out, his shoulders tense but his stride steady as he disappeared down the hall. Something in his silence left me unsettled, wondering what he was thinking.

I tried to ignore the tug of sadness as the door closed behind him. My focus should have been on finding a job, figuring out how to dig myself out from under the weight of my loan. I had agreed to stay just four weeks—until Josephine's checkup next week—and then I'd be free.

And not a moment too soon.

There was no room for distractions, especially the kind Topher could bring.

18

For a woman determined to put distance between herself and a charming billionaire, I certainly hated the distance he put between us the next day. He came home after I went to sleep, and he left before I awoke.

So much for that whole *"I'm not going to work as hard anymore"* speech he gave me on our date on the swan boats. Maybe I was the confused one, because his idea of 'not working as hard' definitely looked like the complete opposite to me.

I missed him. I shouldn't be so angry. I'd wanted distance from him, and he was certainly giving me that distance. But that didn't mean he had to neglect his mom!

By late afternoon, I was more than a little upset. I had no idea where he was or what he was doing, but I could make an educated guess. Some emergency had come up, and instead of trusting his team, he had taken it on himself. That was Topher—always needing to be the one in control, never trusting anyone else to handle it. It was infuriating.

Josephine didn't seem to mind at all. She sat on the couch, her feet propped up, flipping through a magazine like everything was perfectly fine. I paced around the room, trying to figure out how to bring it up without exploding.

Finally, I couldn't hold it in any longer. "Doesn't it bother you?" I blurted out.

Josephine looked up, a soft smile on her face. "What, dear?"

"That he's working when he should be here with you."

"Oh, sweetheart, it's fine. Really, it's fine."

I stopped pacing, my arms crossing over my chest. "How is it fine? You're recovering from surgery, and he's not even around to check on you."

She gave me a patient smile, the kind only a mother could give. "I'm sure he's got his reasons."

Sure, I told him that I wanted distance, but that shouldn't mean that he falls right back into bad habits.

Why couldn't he see how toxic it was to be so obsessed with his work? If this was what life with Topher would look like, I couldn't see a happy future for any woman who chose to be with him.

I'd lived that cycle myself when I was back in college, buried in books and projects, too busy to pick up the phone and call my parents. The guilt still weighed on me, the distance I'd created without even realizing it. I promised myself I'd never go down that path again. And there I was, watching Topher make those same mistakes.

By the time he came back that evening, long after Josephine and I had already eaten dinner, I was ready to explode. Frustration simmered inside me, words bubbling up, ready to burst out. But when I saw him, his shoulders were slumped, exhaustion etched across his face like he was carrying the weight of the world, and I hesitated. Whatever I was about to say died on my lips.

Instead, I closed the distance between us and wrapped my arms around him.

He went still for a moment, then his arms came around me, pulling me close. His chin rested on top of my head, and I felt some of the stiffness leave his body.

"This feels so good," he murmured into my hair. "I could stay like this forever."

"Then let's stay," I whispered back.

And we did. We stood there in the dim light, his heartbeat gradually slowing against my cheek, my hands making small circles on his back. I lost track of how many minutes had passed. His breathing deepened, evened out. The rigid set of his shoulders softened incrementally, like ice melting in the sun.

But when I finally pulled back enough to look up at his face, I could see that edge was still there in his eyes—a tightness at the corners, a wariness that hadn't quite released its hold. The stress had eased, but it hadn't disappeared. It was still lurking, still waiting.

Whatever he was carrying, it wasn't something that could be hugged away.

Later that night, I awoke to the sound of him thrashing in his sleep.

His breath was ragged, his face twisted in pain. Heart pounding, I leaned over the bed to where he was lying on the floor. Gently, I shook his shoulder. "Topher, wake up."

His eyes flew open, wide with panic, and he sucked in a sharp breath, trying to orient himself. Without thinking, I slid to the floor, reaching for him. My arms encircled as much of his broad, tense frame as I could, pulling him close.

"It's okay," I whispered, pressing against him. "You're okay."

He leaned into me, his body trembling as he struggled to steady his breath. After a moment, his voice broke the silence, low and strained. "It's just like the nightmare I used to have when I was younger."

I didn't say anything at first. I just held him, feeling his tension slowly ease under the warmth of my arms. His vulnerability stirred something profound inside me, something protective.

When he spoke, I could feel the rumble of his voice against my neck. "When I was younger, we didn't have enough to eat. My mom was so depressed, and I couldn't do anything about it. I couldn't take care of her." He took a shaky breath. "I still have that nightmare. That I can't take care of the people who are important in my life."

He looked down, ashamed, and it broke my heart to see him like that. He wasn't the invincible billionaire I'd gotten to know; he was a scared kid, terrified of losing the one person who meant everything to him. It hit me then how much he carried on his shoulders, how much of himself he buried beneath the weight of his responsibilities.

Topher's shoulders sagged, and he stared off into the distance for a moment, like he was trying to figure out how to put something into words. Finally, he spoke, his voice low.

"You know why I don't come back here? To New Orleans? To see my mom?" A bitter laugh escaped. "I always say it's because I'm busy with work, and there's too much going on. But that's not the truth."

I stayed quiet, sensing that whatever he was about to say was something he'd been holding onto for a long time.

"The real reason is that I was afraid that the second I walked through the door, I would turn right back into that scared kid again. The one who couldn't fix anything, who didn't know how to take care of his mom. The kid who was terrified of everything falling apart."

He looked down at his hands, his jaw tight. "I thought if I stayed away, kept building my life from a distance, maybe I could leave that kid behind. Pretend I'd grown past all that. And for a while, I believed it. I really did. I'd convinced myself that staying away was helping me stay strong. That I was fine."

He exhaled, shaking his head. "But then this nightmare... It's like the past isn't done with me yet. I've built all this success, but now I'm right back there again."

The pain in his voice tugged at my heartstrings, and I could see how much he'd been holding in, how much of himself he'd wrapped up in this illusion of control. I moved closer, my hand finding his arm, grounding him.

"You're not that child anymore," I said gently. "You can stop running."

He met my gaze, his eyes raw with emotion, and I could see the conflict still playing out there. Then he added, almost too quietly for me to hear, "And I'm scared of failing you."

His words hit me like a jolt, my heart skipping a beat. I pulled back slightly, searching his face. "You won't." My voice was barely above a whisper as I tried to make sense of what he meant. "You won't fail me."

As I held him, the tension slowly eased from his body, his breathing becoming steadier, the panic subsiding. My presence seemed to ground him, calming the storm that had gripped him just moments ago.

Neither of us spoke. We just lay in the quiet, the weight of everything hanging between us. Then, after a long silence, he looked at me, his voice low and raw. "Will you hold me while I fall asleep?"

But letting him in felt like stepping onto dangerous ground. Relying on him, even just for tonight, would make everything feel too real, too raw. And the risk? It was just too high. Because his worst nightmare—failing someone who depended on him—was my worst nightmare, too. His failing me when I needed him the most.

"Of course," I said quietly, willing my voice to stay steady. I figured there was no harm in holding him while he fell asleep, and then I would get back into bed. As long as I didn't sleep next to him, I could protect my heart.

He nodded, and I lay beside him, pulling him into my arms. His makeshift bed on the floor really *was* comfortable.

His body relaxed against mine. With each passing moment, I felt him letting go of the weight he had been carrying for so long.

"You're safe," I murmured, my fingers gently combing through his hair.

He sighed, the sound soft and tired, and there was peace in it. "Thank you," he whispered, his voice so quiet I barely heard it.

His hand found mine, squeezing it lightly, and warmth spread through my chest. I didn't realize how much I needed this, too. How much I needed to be close to him.

But I couldn't let myself fall asleep beside him. I'd drawn a line between us, thin and fragile, but it was there for a reason. Depending on someone like this and feeling safe in their arms, letting down my guard, felt like asking for heartbreak. I knew too well what it meant to lose people, to have them slip away when I thought they'd always be there.

Topher was different, yes, but how could I trust that difference? How could I risk letting myself believe he'd stay, that he wouldn't leave when I needed him most? The thought of relying on him, of letting myself fall into the comfort he offered, was terrifying. I could barely admit it, even to myself, but letting him in meant giving him the power to hurt me, maybe even to shatter me.

Yet, as I held him, his warmth against me, it felt undeniably good. I stayed awake, watching him, listening to his steady breathing as the quiet of the night settled around us.

19

Of course, we fell asleep next to each other.

It wasn't part of the plan—well, not *my* plan—but somewhere in the quiet hours of the night, his arms found their way around me.

At first, I was only half-aware of it. The soft brush of his hand at my waist. The solid weight of his chest rising and falling against my back. His warmth wrapped around me like a blanket, steady and quiet. In my drowsy haze, I didn't resist. I couldn't.

The room was still, lit only by the faint blue glow slipping through the curtains. Outside, a car passed in the distance, tires humming against the street. Inside, the only sound was Topher's breathing—slow and even, like it was tethering me to something I hadn't known I needed.

When morning came, I woke before him. For a few long seconds, I didn't move. His arm was draped across my waist, its weight anchoring me in place. His hand, still lightly curled, rested over my heart.

And my heart—traitorous thing—ached with the sweetness of it.

I knew I should get up. I needed to. His arms felt safe, yes, but *distance* was safer. I couldn't let this become real. I couldn't let it mean something.

But then, in his sleep, he shifted. His arm pulled me closer, not tighter, just... nearer. Like, even unconscious, he didn't want to let go.

And just like that, every reason I had for pulling away disappeared, one by one, until I wasn't sure I remembered any of them at all.

No. I had to wake him up before this went too far. Because I knew exactly how this would end. I'd let myself get close, allow myself to begin to believe that maybe I didn't have to carry everything alone—that maybe someone else could share the load. I'd start to rely on him, and then, when it mattered most, he'd be gone.

It wouldn't happen right away. Maybe not today, or tomorrow, but at some point, he'd leave. Maybe he'd be pulled back into his work, or maybe he'd realize that I wasn't worth staying for. That was the part I couldn't control, the part that terrified me. Because if I let him in, if I let myself depend on him, then I'd be vulnerable. And once he left, I'd be left picking up pieces of myself I wasn't sure I'd be able to put back together.

I'd been here before. I knew the heartache of losing people you'd let yourself depend on. That feeling had shattered me once, and I'd vowed never to let it happen again.

So, no. I couldn't afford to let this feeling deepen, to let myself believe that this could be more than it was. Because when he left—and he would—I'd be right back where I started, but worse.

I leaned in close, feeling the weight of everything I was about to push away, and whispered the first words I could think of that would break the moment. Words that I'd heard Topher say but that meant nothing to me: "Quick, what's our policy on non-compete clauses in international subsidiaries?"

Topher mumbled groggily, "Uh... it depends on the jurisdiction..."

I forced a smirk, trying to lighten my own heavy heart. "Wrong. That's the old policy. We updated it last quarter."

His eyes snapped open, panic flashing across his face. "Wait, what?"

A bittersweet laugh slipped out before I could stop it. "Relax. I'm kidding. You're fine."

He blinked, realizing what had just happened, then let out a groggy chuckle. "Really? That's how you wake me up? You're going to give me a heart attack, you know that?"

I shrugged, still managing a faint smile. "Cruel but effective," I murmured, something warm flickering in my chest even as I fought to ignore it.

Topher smiled, and I watched him for a second, the lines of stress gone from his face. The playful banter was a reminder of why I liked him so much, but its effect on my heart also reminded me why I needed to keep my distance.

He stretched, his eyes finally meeting mine, the smile fading into something more serious. "Last night... thank you." His voice was low, almost hesitant. "For being there for me. I'm glad I didn't have to deal with that alone."

I shrugged, trying to brush it off. "It's nothing, really."

But Topher shook his head. "No. It meant everything." He studied my face for a moment before continuing. "I want to be there for you, too, you know. The way you were there for me."

His arm was still draped over me, a gentle embrace. But his words hit me hard, sinking more deeply into me than I had ever expected they would, and suddenly, the room felt too small, too warm. There was an intimacy in his offer that pressed on a wound I hadn't even realized was still raw. My heart clenched, the vulnerability overwhelming, and I could feel the walls inside me rising, fast and instinctive, to protect myself.

"I'm fine," I said quickly, pulling away from his arm and sitting up, forcing a smile that didn't quite reach my eyes. I shook my head, as if trying to shake off the weight of what he'd said. "I don't need help with anything. Really."

Topher's jaw tightened as he shifted, frustration flashing in his eyes. He sat up, but he didn't look away. "Why are you pushing me away?"

"I'm not," I protested, getting to my feet and walking over to the edge of the bed, needing the distance. But we both knew I was lying. He could see right through it.

He stood slowly, his movements deliberate as he closed the gap I'd just created. He rubbed the back of his neck, hesitating a moment before speaking. "Kathleen, I know you asked for distance, time to focus on yourself without distractions, and I want to give you what you want. But I need you to know... I'm waiting for you. No matter how long it takes, when you're ready, I'm here for you. For us."

Part of me wanted to fall into him right then and there. Another part—the scared part, the self-protective part—tightened its grip. I wasn't used to someone being so romantic. Not for *me*.

Then, in a softer, almost-too-casual tone, he added, "You know, there's an open house for the social work program at Tulane this afternoon. You should go check it out."

I blinked, caught off guard by the shift. "This afternoon? Really?"

"Yeah, I've got some work to do this morning, but my driver can pick you up and take you there."

Excitement flickered inside me, but almost immediately, a wave of nerves followed. The idea of going to the Tulane open house made my stomach twist in knots. I hadn't even finished college. What if I didn't belong there? What if I was wasting everyone's time?

"Your driver?" I raised an eyebrow, trying to mask the mix of excitement and anxiety swirling in my chest. "I don't know... I've never even finished college. What if—"

"Hey." His voice was gentle but firm, cutting through my doubts before they could spiral. "I'll go with you."

I stared at him, the sincerity in his offer catching me completely off guard. *He'd come with me?*

"You'd do that?" I asked, my voice softer than I intended. "You'd come with me?"

"Of course." He shrugged like it was the most obvious thing in the world. "Why wouldn't I?"

My mind buzzed with the weight of his offer, the way he'd so easily volunteered, no hesitation. I wasn't used to someone showing up for me like that. And maybe that's why the knot in my stomach loosened a little.

"I don't know... I didn't expect you to offer," I admitted, my voice tinged with surprise. Part of me wanted to believe I could handle it on my own, but his offer felt like a lifeline I didn't realize I needed.

He gave me a small, reassuring smile. "Well, I'm offering."

As I looked at him, the anxiety didn't disappear entirely, but it softened, replaced by a flicker of hope. Maybe, just maybe, I could go back to school and make something of my life.

"Okay, but you do realize this isn't some fancy gala or board meeting," I teased, crossing my arms. "You'll probably be the only billionaire there."

He laughed, his eyes gleaming with mischief. "Lucky for you, I'm adaptable. I can mingle with the commoners if I have to."

I rolled my eyes. "Commoners, huh? Good luck blending in. Maybe don't tell anyone about your yacht."

"I'll try to keep it under wraps," he teased, his voice dropping as he closed the distance between us. "But you know, I think they'll be more impressed by my charming personality."

"Oh, really?" I raised an eyebrow, trying to keep my tone playful, even as something fluttered in my chest. His closeness was doing things to me that I didn't want to admit.

My breath caught for a moment. His presence felt electric, and before I could think too much about it, he leaned in and gave me a soft kiss. It was quick, but it sent a rush of excitement through me, leaving me stunned—and wanting more.

As he pulled back, Topher smiled, the look on his face so genuine and happy that it made my heart skip a beat. "I'll see you this afternoon. Three-thirty, okay? My driver will pick you up."

Still a little breathless, I nodded, trying to play it cool despite the flutter in my chest. "Three-thirty. Got it."

He gave me a warm look before disappearing into the bathroom. A few minutes later, he re-emerged fully dressed, adjusting the collar of his shirt and slipping on his watch. "I'm looking forward to this," he said, pausing by the doorway, his eyes soft and sincere.

My heart swelled with a hopeful warmth. "Me too."

He shot me one last smile, then headed out, his footsteps fading down the hall. I stood there, holding onto the lingering thrill of his touch, his words, the way he looked at me.

As he smiled and walked out, a flicker of doubt tried to creep in, but I pushed it down, refusing to let it ruin the moment. The excitement still hummed beneath the surface, and I pushed the doubt down, focused on the lingering thrill of his kiss instead.

Turns out, I should have listened to that doubt.

20

I SHOULD'VE KNOWN Topher wouldn't show up.

The driver pulled up right on time at three-thirty, just like Topher had promised, but the back seat? Empty.

"Mr. Brodie's been delayed with work," the driver said, all polite and professional. I forced a smile, nodding as my chest tightened with frustration. *He'd promised.*

I'd spent way too long getting ready for this, changing my outfit at least a dozen times before settling on something that made me feel both confident and professional. And yet, there I was, sitting in an empty car, already deflated before I even arrived.

That was precisely why I shouldn't fall for him. The way his absence reduced me to a simmering, frustrated idiot who was waiting, hoping for something that wasn't coming. It was infuriating. He'd promised, and sure, the tour might seem small to someone else, but it wasn't to me.

The ride to Tulane was a rollercoaster of nerves and barely contained anger. *He didn't even text me.* My brain cycled through every possible excuse he might have, but none of them made me feel better.

I didn't *want* to care this much, but I did. Annoyingly, deeply, I cared. He said he'd be there, and instead, he chose work. Again.

I stared out the window, mentally fast-forwarding through what a future with him would look like. It would be a life of missed dates and canceled plans.

I imagined all the milestones he would miss. *"Your graduation? Totally there... unless there's a last-minute board meeting. You get it, right?"* Or our wedding: *"I have a conference call. So, can I miss the ceremony as long as I make the reception? Or is it the other way around?"*

And kids? Forget about making all their soccer games and dance recitals. *"I know I missed the birth, but hey, I acquired a new company and made a billion dollars while you were pushing, so really, we both achieved something life-changing today."*

I snorted, shaking my head at the ridiculousness of it all. But at least I'd be set for life financially—emotionally neglected, sure—but I wouldn't have to worry about money.

The more I thought about it, the more obvious it became. This was a sign. *Don't fall for him. You can't fall for him.* Because this wasn't about him missing one event—it was about what it meant. It was about broken promises and priorities, and right then, it was clear where I stood.

When we pulled up to Tulane, I hovered at the entrance, doubt gnawing at me. *What am I even doing here?* A college dropout about to walk into a graduate school open house. I almost turned right back around, but something made me stop. I took a deep breath, squared my shoulders, and stepped inside.

To my surprise, the tour was good. Better than good. The more I listened, the more I realized how manageable it all sounded. I could finish my undergraduate degree through their returning-student program and, if I played my cards right, go straight into grad school. The hybrid schedule? That was a game-changer. I wouldn't have to upend my entire life. I could work, study, and find a balance. It wasn't the terrifying leap I'd imagined.

It felt doable.

And then came the real kicker—a fellowship program. It would cover full tuition, plus leave me with enough money to live on while I complete my degree. I felt like a lightbulb had gone off in my head. I could finish school. I could make this happen.

By the end of the tour, I felt lighter, almost hopeful. And all the way back to Josephine's house, I allowed myself to dream. Maybe things were turning around for me.

But as soon as I stepped through the door, my mood soured as I remembered that Topher hadn't been there. Not for me. Not for any of it.

Sinking into the couch, a knot of disappointment tightened in my stomach. I opened my texts, scrolling through, hoping for an apology or an excuse, *anything* to soften the blow of his absence. But there was nothing.

There was no way I could sit there and let the frustration eat me alive, so I headed to the kitchen and started prepping dinner. Maybe chopping vegetables would help me focus on something other than the fact that Topher had stood me up.

I was halfway through slicing an onion when Josephine wandered in. She leaned her hip against the counter. "Well, somebody's having feelings. Should I give y'all a minute? You and the onion seem to be working through something."

I forced a laugh.

Josephine smiled. "Baby, nobody cuts an onion that aggressively unless there's a story."

My shoulders sagged. "I don't have a story."

She tapped the counter twice. "Well, when you feel like telling the story you don't have, I'll be here."

I shrugged. "I needed a distraction."

Josephine peered over my shoulder. "At least you're being productive. I remember one time when I needed a distraction, and I impulsively bought a dozen giant inflatable skeletons. Life-sized, glowing in the dark, each one worse than the last. You can imagine how well *that* went over with the neighbors."

"Skeletons? How did they not chase you out of the neighborhood?"

She smirked. "Oh, I didn't stop at just skeletons. I dressed them up in Saints jerseys and arranged them to march across my lawn like they were in the world's creepiest second-line parade. Complete with trumpets and trombones. And, of course, they played 'When the Saints Go Marching In' on repeat. I was *fully* prepared for angry letters from the HOA when the skeletons wouldn't stop 'marching.'"

"And?"

"And nothing! Instead, one of my neighbors added a zombie referee. Then another neighbor made skeleton fans tailgating on the lawn. It was *spectacular*."

I raised an eyebrow. "Wait, is *that* how your neighborhood's holiday decoration madness started?"

"Yep," she said proudly. "Now it's a full-blown competition. Everyone tries to outdo each other with decorations. I unleashed the beast, and there's no turning back."

"You created a monster," I teased.

Josephine winked. "And I regret nothing."

We continued cooking, the conversation light and playful, Josephine managing to pull me out of my own head for a bit. But every now and then, I'd glance at my phone, sitting on the counter, and still no messages. Each time, the knot in my stomach tightened.

We had just finished dinner, and I was reading a book in bed when the bedroom door swung open. And who should walk in but Topher.

And he was practically glowing with excitement.

Without missing a beat, he crossed the bedroom, sat down beside me, and grabbed my hands, his eyes sparkling like he could barely contain himself. "You'll never believe my news."

21

He had big news? Well, *so did I*.

Okay, not really. But after spending the entire day pacing the house, glaring at my phone, and spiraling into a full-blown emotional meltdown, I felt entitled to *something*.

"You didn't show up today." I tried to keep my voice steady, but inside, I was crumbling.

Topher didn't even blink. "I'm sorry I missed it, but trust me, you'll be glad I did."

I'll be glad? I could feel my frustration bubbling up, ready to spill over. Glad? Let me guess. He bought a sports team? Or an island? Or maybe invented a time machine so he could skip out on more things in the future?

"You didn't even text me to tell me you weren't coming." My voice was sharper than I meant it to be. He looked taken aback, but I didn't care. The words kept spilling out, and there was no stopping them. "You're always working. And I guess I get it. You've got this big, important life. But what about the people in your life, Topher? What about *me*? Was today so insignificant to you? Am I so insignificant to you?"

A small voice inside me whispered that I was right to protect myself. *This is what happens when you let your guard down. This is what happens when you believe in love.* You lose people. I lost my parents, and I wasn't about to let that happen again, not with him. Not with anyone. Because losing someone you love? It's a kind of devastation you can't recover from.

Topher opened his mouth, running his hands through his hair. "I was in the middle of an important meeting. I didn't want to let you down, but I—"

I felt a bitter laugh escape. "You *did* let me down, Topher. But that's the thing. I should've known better." I shook my head, trying to tamp down the devastation rising inside me. That was why I don't trust love. Why I don't believe it can last. Because when you finally let your guard down, that's when people leave. That's when you lose them.

I looked away, blinking back the tears that threatened to spill. "I guess I'm the fool for thinking it would matter to you."

Topher's smile faltered. He looked taken aback, as if I had just deflated whatever news he'd been so excited to share. He opened his mouth to speak, but I wasn't done.

"Your mom's been messing with the Wi-Fi just to get you to take a break, and you're so busy running the world that you didn't even put two and two together!"

"Wait, what?"

I froze, realizing I'd just let the secret slip. His mom had been sabotaging the internet to force him to take breaks, but I hadn't meant to throw her under the bus. I crossed my arms. "Yeah. She doesn't want you working yourself into an early grave."

Topher blinked, clearly thrown off. "She did *what*?"

"I know, shocking, right?" I said, my voice dripping with sarcasm. "But here's the thing, Topher. It doesn't even matter. It's always the same. Work always comes first, no matter what's going on with the people in your life."

He looked at me, stunned by my outburst. He took a deep breath, raising a hand as if to stop me from continuing. "I'm sorry," he said quickly. "But I think you'll be happy once you hear what I have to say."

I froze, the weight of my frustration still brewing beneath the surface, but the sincerity in his voice made me pause.

Topher stepped closer, his eyes locked on mine. "You're right that I've been working. But not for me. I've been working for *you*."

My confusion deepened. He looked so *pleased* with himself as he took both of my hands in his.

"What are you talking about?" I asked.

"I paid off your debt."

My anger faltered, the words not quite registering at first. "My debt?"

He smiled, his eyes gleaming. "It wasn't easy. It took some serious work, and I had to work with our lawyers to make a few changes to the company's bylaws, which is why I've been working nonstop. But it's gone, Kathleen. You're free of it."

I blinked, still trying to process. "You... paid off my debt?"

He nodded, and his smile grew even wider, as if he'd just handed me the world. "Yeah. It's gone. No more penalties, no more interest. Everything's wiped clean."

I stood there, my mind struggling to catch up. How was this even possible? Could a billionaire just wave a magic wand and make things disappear? It didn't make sense. Could he just change the bylaws of any company he wanted? Was that how the world worked?

"How?" I asked, skepticism thick in my voice. "How did you get them to waive the rule that I couldn't pay it back early?"

He hesitated for just a second, his eyes locking onto mine. "Because I own the company."

For a moment, the air seemed to thicken around us, the weight of his words not quite hitting me entirely yet. "You what?"

"I own the loan company. The one that holds your debt," he said slowly, his voice soft, as if he were easing me into this reality.

I took a step back, my pulse racing, the pieces starting to fall into place. *I own the company.* The same loan company that had made my life so difficult for years. The one that bought my parents' debt and had been steadily growing it, trapping me under a mountain of financial ruin.

I was frozen, as the shock gave way to a slow-burning anger. All those years of struggling under the weight of that debt, the fear of never getting out from under it. I couldn't breathe. I couldn't think. This was the company that had made my life so hard.

And Topher had been behind it all.

22

It felt like I'd been punched in the chest.

Topher was still smiling, as if he'd given me the best news in the world, completely unaware of the weight of what he'd just revealed.

I swallowed, my voice tight with disbelief. "You own the loan company? The one that's been harassing me for years? The reason I dropped out of college? The company that bought out my parents' debt and has been increasing it? *That* company?"

Topher's smile faltered, confusion flickering in his eyes. "Yes, that's my company." He spoke slowly, cautiously, now, like he was realizing this wasn't the celebration he thought it would be.

My mind was spinning, flashing back to the endless stress: the sleepless nights, the mounting fear, the suffocating pressure of trying to escape that debt.

Shock crashed over me like a wave. I pulled my hands out of his, my skin suddenly feeling too hot. "You're telling me you own the company that's been dragging me down for *years*?"

He wasn't quite so confident anymore, and his voice took on a defensive tone. "It's a huge company. We handle debt for millions of people. I had no idea you were one of them."

The room seemed to shrink around me, the walls closing in. "So, you've been profiting off my misery this whole time?"

Topher's eyes widened, as if the shock finally dawned on him. He took a step forward, his expression pleading. "No, it's not like that—"

"But it *is*." I was shaking, the anger rising in my chest. "I've been drowning in this debt, and all along, you were behind the company, pulling the strings!"

His shoulders drooped, and he reached out to me again. "As soon as I found out, I moved heaven and earth to fix it. I swear. I paid it off because I care about you. I just wanted to make it right."

Moved heaven and earth? Oh, please. The $150,000 in debt that was world-shattering and future-crushing to me was probably pocket change to him. A tiny fraction of his net worth. He could've paid it off in the time it takes to order coffee. He didn't make some grand, heroic effort. It was nothing. A blip on his radar, easily erased. And now, he stood there, acting like he'd just solved all my problems with a wave of his billionaire wand. Like I should be grateful.

But I wasn't. I couldn't be. This wasn't just about the debt. It was about everything that debt represented. That debt had been the secret my parents kept from me, something so massive they couldn't bring themselves to share it. And then, when they were gone, I was left to deal with its crushing weight. Finding out how deep in debt they were, how much they'd hidden from me, was devastating. It didn't just wreck my life financially; it shattered my trust and my sense of stability. And now, the man sitting next to me, the man I had fallen for, had been part of it all along.

I ran, storming down the hall toward the front of the house. I needed air, and I needed to escape the weight of what he'd just told me.

"Kathleen, wait," he said, catching up to me. His voice was pleading, desperate. "You don't understand. I don't work with individual cases. I run the company, so I have no idea who has what debt within it. I thought paying off your debt would help."

"Help?" I spun around. "That company—your company—has made my life miserable for years. It destroyed everything my parents worked for and left me with nothing but heartache. And I'm not the only one. There are so many others out there just like me. Even if my debt is gone, what about them? How can I even think about being with someone who's part of that?"

The man I had fallen for had been a part of it all along. And I had fallen for him, so it didn't matter how much I tried to pretend I was still safe. I was so far from safe. I was already torn to pieces.

His face fell, but then his jaw tightened, his eyes flashing with frustration. "It's not all bad. My company isn't some heartless machine. Or, at least it wasn't at first. I started it right after graduating from Brown. I wanted to help people. If something like it had been around when my mom and I were struggling, we might not have lost our house."

I crossed my arms, still skeptical. "What exactly was it supposed to do?"

He took a deep breath. "It was designed to give people in debt options. I wanted it to be different, offering features like personalized payment plans, budgeting tools, and even financial counseling. The goal was to work with people, not just to hunt them down. I wanted to give people a second chance, a way out."

"So what changed?"

Topher's smile faded, guilt creeping into his expression. "It grew fast. Faster than I'd ever planned. Once investors came in, there was pressure to maximize profit, and before I knew it, we had entire teams dedicated solely to collections." He hesitated, his voice softer, as if he were seeing the impact for the first time. "I tried to balance what I originally wanted with what the business had become, but I kept choosing to expand, to push for more growth. I could've scaled back or restructured, but I convinced myself I could do both. That I could help people and still keep the company thriving."

He looked up, eyes clouded with regret. "Somewhere along the way, I forgot that there were real people behind those loans. It all became numbers on a page."

Tears started falling from my eyes, and I didn't even wipe them away. "You're tied to all the memories I've been trying to run from. My parents hid how deep in debt they were, and then they died and left me with it. And now you're just another person who's been lying to me—whether you meant to or not."

He stepped closer, his voice softening. "I never wanted to lie to you. I was trying to fix it."

I shook my head, backing away from him. "But you can't. How can I be with you when you're tied to all these memories now? Memories I can't escape."

Topher reached out, gently placing his hand on my arm. His touch was soft, almost hesitant, as if he were afraid I might slip away completely. "But what we have... You can't just walk away from that."

My heart ached, torn between the pull I felt toward him and the fears that kept me grounded. "I agreed to stay until your mom got better," I said, forcing each word out, the pain pressing against my chest. "It's been almost four weeks, and she's better now. It's time for me to leave."

I couldn't look at him, but I could feel the weight of his gaze. His voice was low, filled with concern. "Where are you going to stay? You could stay at my place in the Garden District. Or... I could rent you a place, maybe even buy you something small if that's what you need."

My cheeks burned, a mixture of embarrassment and frustration rising in me. "No," I snapped. "That's not what I need. I thought you didn't believe in charity. But here I am, your charity case. I'm glad you finally found the giving impulse, but I don't want to be your project."

He shook his head, pain flashing across his face. "This isn't charity. It's... It's what you do when you care about someone."

My heart twisted, tangled up in the anger and hurt, but also in a hard truth I couldn't ignore. I looked at him, steeling myself. "It can't work, Topher. We're too different." I spoke quietly, shaking my head. "This... whatever this was, it would never work."

"How can you say that?"

I swallowed hard, pushing down the pull I felt toward him. "We started with lies, Topher. And now that I know who you really are—what you do, how you earn your money—I see the truth."

His voice was softer now. "You can't tell me that what we have is just nothing. That the moments we've shared, the way we challenge each other, the way we *fit*—that none of that matters."

"You don't understand," I said, voice barely a whisper. "I can't live wondering if I'll be the next thing you don't have time for."

"I *am* here," he said, his voice fierce. "And if I've fallen short, I'll fight every day to prove to you that you can count on me." He searched my face, frustration and longing in his gaze. "If this is about the mistakes I've made, then let me fix them. But don't shut me out just because it's easier to push me away than let yourself be vulnerable."

A lump formed in my throat as I admitted my fear. It held me back, and I couldn't ignore that. The crushing disappointment of him not showing up when he'd promised, the shock of finding out he owned the very loan that had haunted me for years—each of these felt like proof that every time I let someone in, I ended up more hurt than before.

"I've spent years picking up the pieces of other people's decisions," I said. "I can't do it again. I can't be with someone who might break me."

Topher's hand tightened around mine, his voice almost a whisper. "I'm not walking away, Kathleen. Not unless you look me in the eye and tell me you feel *nothing*."

I closed my eyes, feeling the ache, the longing, the fear. *Of course* it wasn't nothing. But that didn't change the reality I couldn't ignore.

"Topher..." My voice was barely audible.

He stepped closer, his voice a plea. "Don't leave because you're afraid. Let me show you that we can make this work."

His words wrapped around me, tugging at the walls I'd so carefully built. I wanted to believe him, to let myself lean on someone else, to trust that this time it would be different. But I was too afraid.

I took a shaky breath, my heart aching. "I want to believe you, Topher. I do." I swallowed hard, the words tearing at me. "I want this. But I can't... I just can't. Please... let me go."

Topher's face fell, the hurt clear in his eyes. He held my gaze for a moment, his voice barely above a whisper. "If that's really what you want." He slowly released my hand, stepping back as if he was finally accepting it. "I'll... I'll sleep on the couch out here."

If that's really what you want. The words hit me like a slap, each syllable digging in. This was what I'd chosen, wasn't it? This was what I wanted: to be free of the risk and to keep myself safe. As he turned away, a hollow ache settled in my chest. I wanted nothing more than to call him back, but I knew that for now, this was the choice I had to make.

That night, I packed my things slowly, each piece I folded reminding me that this was the right choice, even if it didn't feel like it. I stuffed clothes into my bag as quietly as I could, my hands moving mechanically while my mind raced.

I stayed up for hours, glancing toward the door, half-tempted to leave then and there. But something kept me rooted, watching the faint glow of dawn creep into the room. It was easier this way, I told myself. If I left before anyone was awake, I could skip the painful goodbyes.

When I went into the living room that morning, Topher was sleeping on the couch, the morning light catching the edge of his jaw. I felt a pang deep in my chest.

I tightened my grip on my bag, the weight of my decision dragging every step. Without looking back, I turned and headed for the door, my heart clenching with each inch that took me further from him.

As I slipped out, the door gently closed behind me. The air was calm, quiet, and undisturbed.

This was the right choice. The only choice. The only way to protect myself from falling apart *when* he left.

Because he would.

If Topher could abandon the values on which he built his company, what was stopping him from abandoning me? No matter what promises he made, I couldn't afford to believe them. Not when the cost could be *me.*

23

THE WEEKS BLURRED TOGETHER. Days stretched into one another, a hazy mix of work, routine, and quiet avoidance. Every morning felt like dragging myself up from the bottom of a lake, the weight on my chest sinking deeper with each passing day.

I needed a job, something to keep my mind occupied and my wallet from running dry, so I found one at the coffee shop that Josephine had told me about, called Brewed Awakening. No experience required, daily pay, and enough hours to help me scrape together rent for a tiny apartment along the streetcar line.

Unfortunately, everything reminded me of Topher.

And I do mean everything.

A well-dressed customer walked in, nodding politely to me. Of course, he was wearing a suit. Just like Topher always did, looking perfectly polished even when he was doing something simple, like pouring a glass of water. My heart did a ridiculous little flip as I made the guy's order.

I turned to the milk station, grabbing a jug as usual, but as I poured, another memory surfaced. *Only whole milk*, Topher would say. *None of this skim nonsense.* I felt my chest tighten. *Get a grip*, I told myself, but that didn't stop the ache.

A mother with her toddler approached, and I handed her a napkin along with her coffee. I could practically see Topher then, setting the table with meticulous care, one napkin at each place.

Then came the music. The speakers crackled to life with *Total Eclipse of the Heart,* and I nearly dropped a cup. Right on cue, a memory of Topher in Josephine's kitchen, lip syncing while he stirred pasta, hit me like a punch.

I sighed, setting a fresh latte on the counter, the weight of everything pressing down on me. I was exhausted—tired of feeling hollow, of seeing ghosts of Topher in every coffee cup, every napkin, every faint echo of a song. The ache of it all had wound itself around my heart.

Then, a magazine on the counter caught my eye, one of those glossy entertainment rags. In the bottom corner of the cover, I spotted a guy who looked eerily like Topher. Fantastic. As if I weren't already haunted by reminders of him in every corner of my life. I leaned in for a closer look, and my stomach dropped. No way. It *was* Topher, arm casually draped around Hollywood's latest "It" girl, Serena Blake, both of them smiling.

The headline screamed: "Is Serena Blake Dating Billionaire Financier?"

My heart did a painful backflip, then shattered into a thousand pieces right there in my chest.

Of course he'd moved on—and with a Hollywood star, no less. They were probably jet-setting around the world in matching private planes, hers lined with designer pet carriers, his stocked with his erg machine. I could picture them lounging on some private island, sipping drinks out of coconuts carved with their initials, laughing at how quaint "normal" people were.

She'd bring out her latest script, and they'd debate whether the billionaire in her movie should drive the red Ferrari or the black one.

Maybe they'd host charity galas together, cooing over the endangered alpacas they were "saving"—all for the tax break, naturally. Topher wasn't one to give anyone a leg up out of the goodness of his heart.

I should feel relieved. Or, at the very least, certain that I'd made the right choice. But there I was, four weeks since I'd last seen Topher, serving coffee to strangers, and every little thing still brought him rushing back to me. I'd walked away thinking it would bring me peace and give me the control I'd been desperate for. Instead, I felt hollow, as if I'd left a part of myself behind, something I couldn't shake, no matter how much I tried to convince myself that I had done the right thing.

I missed him. And not just the big things, like his ridiculous, over-confident pep talks or the way he'd look at me like he could see right through the walls I kept up. It was the little things. The gifts he thought would "improve my day," like an obnoxiously bright yellow notebook because he'd read somewhere that yellow "boosts creativity." Or that stubborn crease between his eyebrows when he was trying to solve every problem all at once.

And, somehow, in those small details, the ache was worse. Because those were the things that weren't supposed to matter, right? The things that shouldn't be clawing at me. But there I was, hearing a song he once sang, imagining him in every business-suited customer I saw, wishing I could turn and see him grinning at me, like none of this had ever happened.

My mind kept slipping back to him. He and Josephine watching *Jeopardy!* And I'd missed Halloween. I could almost picture him in some ridiculous costume handing out candy. Had the littlest trick-or-treaters liked Josephine's haunted decorations, or were they too scared to come to the door? I felt a pang thinking of her, too.

I leaned my elbows on the counter, staring out at the rain, half-expecting some montage to play in my head, full of poignant moments reminding me why I'd walked away. But instead, all I felt was this ache, a quiet sadness I couldn't shake. I should've felt stronger, freer. But the truth was, I couldn't stop replaying all the silly, annoying, wonderful things he'd done.

I was wiping down the counter when I saw Josephine standing just inside the door. My heart skipped a beat, a knot of surprise and dread twisting in my stomach. I caught my manager's eye, and she gave me a quick nod to take a break. I slipped off my apron, made two lattes, and joined Josephine at a quiet corner table.

We sat in silence for a moment, the steam from our cups swirling between us. I wasn't sure what to say, so I just waited, sipping my coffee and hoping she couldn't feel the tension radiating off me.

She broke the silence, her voice soft, without a trace of anger. "I would have come to see you sooner, you know, but... I didn't know where you'd moved. Not until I found out you were working at this coffee shop I love."

My chest tightened, and I felt my throat go dry. "I'm sorry. I didn't mean to leave without saying goodbye..." Such a weak attempt at explaining myself. Not even worth finishing the sentence.

But Josephine reached across the table and squeezed my hand. "You don't have to explain, sweetheart. I just wanted to check on you and see how you're doing."

The warmth in her voice was like a lifeline, and I found myself finally breathing a little easier. "I'm, uh, good." I sounded steadier, but my heart was pounding.

Josephine offered a small, sad smile that twisted my stomach. She took a breath, then leaned forward. "I also wanted to talk to you about Topher. I thought you'd want to know about the trouble with his company."

Her words felt like a splash of ice water down my spine. I tried to nod, forcing myself to appear calm. "I hadn't heard anything."

She gave me a long, assessing look, then let out a sigh. "His financiers are forcing him out. Apparently, he paid off some debt early. It was a tiny amount, compared to the company's net worth, but it broke the company's bylaws, and now they're using it against him." She shook her head.

"He never trusted those partners and felt like they were always looking for a way to replace him and get the power for themselves. It's sad because that company meant so much to him. He poured his life into it."

I swallowed, feeling her words settle as the pieces started to click into place. *Debt.* I could feel the blood drain from my face as it dawned on me: He'd done it for me.

I struggled to process the weight of what she was saying. My heart dropped. Topher's words came flooding back—how he'd told me he'd "moved heaven and earth" to cover my debt, and I'd scoffed, convinced he was exaggerating. But he'd been telling the truth. He'd risked everything for me.

Josephine's gaze softened as she looked down at her cup, her fingers tracing the edge. "He's been building that company since he was young, before he had anything to his name. It's more than just a business to him; it's his legacy, his proof to himself and everyone else that he could do something meaningful, something lasting." She paused, her voice tinged with sadness. "Losing it now, I don't know what he'll do."

She continued, her voice a little quieter, almost hesitant. "He's gone back to New York, you know. He's gone."

It felt like I'd been punched in the chest. *Gone.* He was really gone. So the magazine was right.

I was silent, and Josephine just looked at me, as if she were expecting something more. "Anyway, I didn't come here to burden you with all this," she said, her voice gentler. "I don't know everything that happened between you two, but I wanted to see how you're holding up. I'm sure it's been a tough road for you also."

I swallowed hard, forcing myself to smile, though it felt like a lie. "I'm... good," I murmured, even as the ache in my chest twisted tighter.

She reached across the table, placing her hand on mine. "Losing both of your parents so young leaves a mark. You carry that fear with you, don't you? Afraid that if you let people in, you might lose them too."

The truth of her words cut deep. I'd always tried to keep that fear hidden. I'd pushed Topher away, driven by a need to protect myself from exactly this—this ache, this feeling of being left alone again. But in the end, my own fear had caused the very thing I'd wanted to avoid.

As I sat across from Josephine, her hand still resting on mine, a strange sense of calm settled over me, though my heart was racing beneath it. She studied me with that motherly gaze of hers, her eyes filled with understanding.

"You've been through so much on your own. I can't imagine how hard it must have been, but... sometimes, we can only carry that weight for so long before it starts pulling us under."

Since my parents died, I'd spent so long building walls, protecting myself, convinced I'd be safer alone. But had I protected myself from anything, or had I just made it harder to let anyone in?

I forced a smile, feeling that familiar ache in my chest. "I just... I don't like the idea of letting down my guard, you know?"

She nodded, squeezing my hand. "Sometimes we think we're protecting ourselves by keeping everything closed off. But the truth is, Kathleen, facing what scares us is often the only way to set ourselves free."

I felt the weight of her words settling in, and for some reason, my mind drifted to the dusty box in my closet—the one with all the papers and letters I hadn't dared to open since my parents died. I'd told myself I wasn't ready to see whatever I might find.

Josephine's gaze softened, and she offered me a gentle smile. "You deserve peace. You deserve to let go of whatever's keeping you locked up inside."

A lump rose in my throat, and I forced myself to speak. "I miss you."

We stood, and she leaned over and wrapped me in a hug, her warmth filling the empty spaces I'd been carrying around for weeks. "I miss you too, sweetheart. You became like a daughter to me, you know. I hope we can stay in touch, and that you find the peace you're looking for."

I watched her turn and walk away, each step taking her farther until she disappeared down the street.

I had pushed Topher away. I made this happen. And now he was with a Hollywood star who fit perfectly into his world, someone who was probably everything I wasn't.

It was over. He was gone. And I had no one to blame but myself.

24

SOMETHING SHIFTED inside me after I talked with Josephine. It wasn't exactly hope, but a shaft of light cutting through the fog I'd been lost in, a small sign that maybe, just maybe, I didn't have to keep feeling hollow.

I was tired of feeling empty, of spending each day locked inside the prison I'd built for myself. I was finally beginning to understand that I had chosen this isolation, the wall I'd kept around my heart. I'd thought I'd been protecting myself, but all I'd done was ensure my own misery.

Josephine made me realize that I'd pushed Topher away because I'd been terrified of needing someone, of being let down, of losing him the way I'd lost everyone else. Losing my parents had taught me a brutal lesson about love and trust, one I'd taken too far. When they'd left me with nothing but debt and unanswered questions, I'd learned to rely only on myself, to fear letting anyone close enough to leave a mark.

But this hollow feeling wasn't protection; it was a punishment. And I was doling it out to myself.

To grow, I had to confront the very things I'd been avoiding—my parents' legacy and the mountain of debt they'd left behind. Maybe it was time to finally dig through that box of paperwork, to come to terms with whatever secrets lay buried there.

I couldn't ignore that they'd left me in a mess. The anger and distrust I'd felt when I discovered the debt still sat heavy in my chest. They'd loved me, I knew that, but what kind of love leaves a daughter burdened and blindsided? It felt like a betrayal, even if I could never admit it.

After I got off my shift at the coffee shop, I dragged myself back to my tiny apartment. I slumped onto the worn-out couch, staring at the cardboard box I had pulled out of the closet. It was battered, taped together at the corners, and marked with my mother's handwriting. Her careful script labeled it "Important Papers." I'd avoided this box for years, but now, here it was, staring back at me like it had been waiting for this moment.

I took a deep breath, my fingers trembling as I reached for the lid. Inside, stacks of papers were arranged neatly. Legal forms, bank statements, and bits of my family's history lay tucked into old envelopes, yellowed at the edges. I forced myself to dig through them, trying not to overthink each page, each memory.

Beneath one envelope was a photo, one I hadn't seen in years. The three of us on move-in day at Duke, standing by the car with ear-to-ear smiles. They'd been so proud, and I'd been so grateful, knowing they'd saved all their lives to make this possible. It had been our dream, and they'd given me everything they had to help me achieve it.

What had happened?

And then, toward the bottom, I noticed a small envelope addressed to me in my mother's familiar handwriting. I hesitated, letting my fingers trace over the letters, as if touching that ink could somehow bring her back. Memories came flooding in, of her warm hugs and my dad's booming laughter, the feeling of home that was now just a hollow ache.

I'd seen the envelope a hundred times before, but I'd never had the courage to open it.

With a shaky breath, I finally tore it open, unfolding a single sheet of paper. The typed lines were precise and formal, devoid of any warmth. The cold, official facts spilled across the page. As I read, my breath caught. It detailed debts, loans, and the overwhelming burden my parents had carried in silence.

The document explained everything I hadn't known. My mother had faced a sudden heart condition a few years before their deaths. Doctors had found a blocked artery, and only a complex, high-risk surgery had offered her a chance. At the time, I'd just started my first year at Duke. I knew about the surgery, of course, but I didn't know that they'd taken out loans for her treatment, intending to pay it all back on their own. But life had other plans, and they'd died in the accident, leaving me with a stack of legal papers and a lifetime of unanswered questions.

I blinked back tears, rereading the cold, clinical phrases, letting the truth settle in. All these years, I'd resented them, convinced they'd left me burdened without a second thought. But now, holding this document, I could see it clearly. They'd done it out of love, out of a fierce need to protect me—even if things hadn't gone as they'd planned.

The resentment I'd held onto so tightly began to unravel, piece by piece, leaving room for something else. Something closer to forgiveness.

I couldn't stop myself from wishing I still had the locket with their picture in it. It had been my last tangible piece of them, and losing it felt like losing them all over again.

If only I hadn't been so careless. The small silver heart had been my way of carrying them with me, a quiet reminder of the life I once had. Without it, I felt as though there was this emptiness that even my memories couldn't quite fill. I'd lost so much already, and holding onto something as simple as that locket might have made these moments feel a little less lonely.

I leaned back on my worn-out couch, fingers still tingling from rifling through years of my parents' hidden truths, touching papers they had once held, choices they'd made out of necessity and shielding me out of love. The morning sun streamed through the window, soft and warm, washing the room in a light that felt almost... hopeful. But as the truth settled in, the weight of it all broke over me, and I couldn't hold it in any longer.

Tears slipped down my cheeks, one after another, until I was crying fully, my chest shaking with the release. The grief, the anger, and the loneliness that had been bottled up inside me were finally breaking free. For the first time, I let myself mourn everything I'd lost and everything I hadn't understood until now. And as I cried, piece by piece, I could feel the weight lift, the years of resentment melting away as I finally grasped what my parents had done for me, and why they'd kept it all hidden.

In their absence, I'd spent years building walls, believing they would protect me from pain, from loss, from the hollow feeling that seemed to settle deeper with every passing year. But I saw it now, how those walls had only kept me locked away from anything real. By pushing Topher away, I'd denied myself the chance to truly heal, to open myself up to something good. My reluctance to accept help didn't make me strong; it just made me lonely. I'd been afraid that leaning on someone, accepting love, would somehow make me weaker. But I was beginning to understand that it could actually make me stronger.

Still, the thought of Topher's face on that magazine cover lingered in my mind, a bitter reminder of what I'd given up. He'd moved on. Of course, he had. He was Topher Brodie. I'd had my chance, and I'd pushed it away.

But that didn't mean I couldn't start over. I'd finally gone through my parents' papers and faced the pain I'd buried for so long, and now, maybe, I could go on with the rest of my life without dragging the past behind me.

I closed my eyes, feeling the sun soak into my skin. I let myself believe that I could choose something different. If I wanted more than this half-life, I'd have to be willing to let someone in, to take that risk, even if it hurt.

My future was waiting for me.

Taking a deep breath, I pulled out my phone. I hesitated for just a second before scrolling to a name I hadn't thought about in a while: Mr. Five Hours Early. I'd met him the same fateful day I'd met Topher, when he was my passenger on the airport shuttle.

I dialed his number, my heart pounding a little faster.

When he picked up, I cleared my throat. "Hey. Could I buy you a coffee?"

25

I SHUFFLED OUT OF CLASS, balancing a cup of coffee in one hand and a stack of notebooks in the other. I spotted Dr. Andersen—Mr. Five Hours Early himself—waiting near the door with his usual, slightly over-eager grin.

Ever since he'd written my recommendation letter, he'd become something of a guardian angel, though one who believed the key to life was "always arriving ten minutes early."

Somehow, he'd taken it upon himself to guide me through my entire Tulane journey, urging me toward the best study spots, quietly checking in after classes, and constantly reminding me of campus resources.

I'd spent years wearing my independence like a badge, proud of handling things on my own. But when I finally let myself ask for help, Dr. Andersen was there without hesitation. And then, as if I'd somehow activated a support network I didn't know I had, others started stepping in too.

There was Larry from the DMV. I hadn't seen him in years. Not since that time I helped him figure out how to finally renew his fishing license without accidentally canceling his driver's license (don't ask). Somehow, he heard through the grapevine that I needed a place to stay, and the next thing I knew, he was renting me an old studio for practically nothing. It came with a suspiciously creaky floorboard, but hey, it was home, and it was near Tulane.

And then there was Mrs. Patel from the grocery store. I casually mentioned that I was looking for a car, and within a day, she'd called up a distant cousin and worked her magic, scoring me a deal on a slightly rattly but reliable Camry. All I had to do was agree to drop by for tea occasionally and listen to her latest theories about grocery store price conspiracies.

As I headed down the familiar path to my apartment, sorting through the stack of mail I'd just picked up, a glossy, oversized envelope slipped out. It was heavier than the rest, and I stopped mid-step, holding it up in the fading light. Embossed in silver were the words *Bright Futures Foundation Gala.* My heart stuttered.

I frowned, flipping it over to see if it was some kind of mistake. Bright Futures. The charity I'd been so passionate about—the one I'd tried to convince Topher to support. But who would be inviting me to their big, high-end gala?

I looked around, half-expecting someone to jump out and yell *surprise!* as if this were all some elaborate prank. But it was just me, standing in the middle of the sidewalk, clutching this invitation as if it might disappear. I couldn't help but wonder: why me?

Peeling open the envelope, I pulled out a thick card. It had all the details laid out in elegant script. There would be a cocktail hour, a three-course dinner, and a lineup of some of the city's top philanthropists. There was even a note saying it was black tie, which might as well have been code for *you don't belong here.*

I shook my head, bewildered. Who would've thought to send me this?

As I turned the invitation over in my hands, something on the back caught my eye. Scrawled in barely legible ink were a few words: *I hope to see you here. Topher*

I felt my breath hitch, recognizing the familiar, messy handwriting. Topher. He'd sent this. *He wanted me there.* I swallowed, emotions swirling through me as I traced the words with my thumb.

My curiosity flaring, I pulled out my phone and looked up Bright Futures Foundation. The first article that popped up took me by surprise. It was recent, reporting that the foundation had just received a massive, anonymous donation. A donation so large that it had completely transformed what was possible for the charity. The article mentioned plans for new youth programs, expanded scholarship funds, and resources for families in crisis, all of which were made possible thanks to this mysterious donor. It was clear that the foundation was on the verge of becoming something extraordinary.

As I scrolled down the article, a line caught my eye, something that stopped me cold.

"The anonymous donor shared a personal motivation for the gift, quoting a conversation that shaped his perspective: 'Someone important to me once told me that when the bills pile up, it can feel like your dreams are slipping away. That's why I did this.'"

My heart squeezed, feeling that familiar sting of bittersweet memories. Topher had listened. I could still remember that day, telling him all the things I'd kept bottled up, not knowing how close he'd been listening.

A small, nervous smile spread across my face. He'd poured his resources into something I cared about deeply, maybe more than he could've guessed. He hadn't just listened. He'd acted.

My pulse quickened as I looked down at the invitation again, his handwritten note lifting my spirits to a place I'd forgotten. *I hope to see you here.* It was just a few simple words, yet they had the power to pull me in a thousand directions at once.

Part of me wanted to tuck the invitation away, bury it at the bottom of a drawer, pretend I'd never seen it. The thought of seeing Topher again—of risking all those feelings I'd worked so hard to push down—was terrifying. What if he'd moved on completely? What if I showed up, and it meant nothing to him?

But then my eyes went back to the article about the donation to

Bright Futures. He'd listened, taken my words, and turned them into something tangible. All those conversations we'd had, the fears I'd let slip, he'd heard every one of them. And he'd acted on them in a way that left me feeling both touched and seen.

I held the invitation a little tighter, my heart battling with my head.

The easy thing would be to stay home. There was safety in keeping my distance.

But I'd spent so long keeping people at arm's length, afraid to be vulnerable, always trying to protect myself from hurt. If I didn't take this chance, if I didn't let myself believe, I'd be doing exactly what I'd done for so long: closing myself off, choosing the easy way out.

This time was different. I'd grown. I'd learned how to ask for help, how to accept it. I'd taken steps toward a new life, made it on my own when I'd thought I couldn't. And maybe this was the final step. I needed to show up, even if it meant risking the pain all over again.

I took a deep breath. As the tremor of fear started to fade, something else took its place: determination. I wasn't the same person I'd been when I met Topher. This wasn't about me proving something to him. This was about me proving something to myself: that I was brave enough to show up, that I could open myself to possibility, to love, without fear of what might happen.

I would go. I'd face the unknown, show up in that ballroom, and let him see the person I'd become. This was my grand gesture. I chose to believe, to hope, and to be vulnerable. I didn't know what would happen, but I knew I had to try.

THAT'S how I ended up in a borrowed ball gown two weeks later, my hair twisted into an elegant updo and a nervous flutter in my stomach that hadn't settled since I'd walked through the doors. The Audubon Tea Room was buzzing, chandeliers casting a warm glow over the elegant guests who glided through the room with champagne glasses in hand, their laughter floating above the music. I took a steadying breath, scanning the crowd, half-expecting Topher to appear any second, his eyes meeting mine across the room, just like I'd pictured a dozen times since I got the invitation.

And then, there he was.

Across the room, looking as polished as ever in a tuxedo. I froze, breath catching, waiting for him to notice me, to give me that look that always seemed like it was meant just for me.

Then, he raised his eyes and caught mine. The air between us seemed to shift, to charge. A spark passed between us. I could feel it. *I knew he felt it too.*

My heart thudded as he started toward me, his gaze never leaving mine. He moved through the crowd like it wasn't even there, like I was the only person in the room.

When he reached me, he stopped. Just stopped and stared.

"Kathleen," he breathed, his voice barely audible over the music. His eyes traveled over me slowly, taking me in. "You look..." He shook his head, a small, almost disbelieving smile tugging at his lips. "You're absolutely stunning."

Heat rushed to my cheeks. "Thank you," I managed, my voice coming out softer than I intended. I tried not to sound like I was winded from *standing still.*

He stepped closer, close enough that I could smell his cologne, feel the warmth radiating from him. "I mean it," he said, his voice dropping lower, more intimate. "I knew you'd be beautiful, but this..." His eyes held mine, something intense and unguarded flickering in their depths. "You took my breath away."

Before I could respond, he leaned in. His lips brushed my cheek, lingering longer than necessary.

The world tilted.

That simple touch sent a rush of sensation through me, like every nerve ending had suddenly come alive. My breath hitched. I felt the shiver run through him too, the way his hand tightened slightly on my arm, the way he went very still.

When he pulled back, his eyes had darkened, that careful control he always maintained suddenly precarious.

"Kathleen," he said again, my name rough on his tongue.

Then his phone buzzed in his pocket. His thumb hovered like he might respond to whatever was buzzing, then dropped without typing. "Sorry."

I gave him a soft smile. "You couldn't take one night off?"

"Oh, it's not work," he murmured, shooting another glance at the phone. "But it is important."

My heart sank. What could be so important?

Then the emcee's voice rang out: "Let's hear it for Mr. Topher Brodie!"

Topher rolled his eyes. "Here we go."

"What's happening?" I asked.

He stepped back, reluctantly. "I may have agreed to auction off a date."

"A date?"

"For charity," he added, as if that made this less bizarre.

I stared at him. "You're being auctioned off?"

"I panicked. My mom signed me up before surgery." He grimaced. "She said if I survived, I had to do something 'fun and humiliating.' Her words."

"And you're just... going along with it?"

He looked at me again. "I'd rather be talking to you."

I opened my mouth to say something, but before I could, a cheerful voice boomed over the speakers. The band switched to a lively tune, and the emcee took the stage, tapping the microphone with a mischievous grin. "Ladies and gentlemen, it's time for our charity auction! Tonight, we have a very special item up for bid—a date with one of the most eligible bachelors in the world, the very man who made this entire evening possible: Mr. Topher Brodie!"

Topher's name echoed through the ballroom, followed by a roar of applause. He winced and took a step back. "Don't go anywhere," he said, eyes locked on mine. "Please."

I nodded, too stunned to do anything else.

Then he turned and walked onto the stage, every eye following him. For a second, his eyes found mine in the crowd, lingering just long enough to make my heart skip. Then, he gave a polite wave to the audience, his expression calm and composed, like this was all perfectly normal. I gripped my clutch tightly, feeling the sting of embarrassment prickling at the back of my neck.

The emcee leaned into the microphone with a grin. "All proceeds going to Bright Futures, of course. So who's ready to take a chance on love—and philanthropy?"

A chorus of enthusiastic cheers rose from the crowd. One woman yelled, "I'll start the bidding at five hundred!"

Another called out, "Make it a thousand!"

Topher chuckled, glancing at the audience, but when his eyes met mine, he hesitated. My heart leaped. But he looked away quickly, giving a polite smile to a woman who'd just yelled, "Two thousand!"

The emcee's voice boomed over the laughter, "Looks like we've got some fierce competition tonight, folks."

Paddles shot up around the room, and my heart sank as the bids climbed higher and higher. I watched in disbelief as he stood on stage, completely unfazed, nodding politely as the emcee read off each bid with mounting excitement.

"Four thousand!" shouted a woman in a sequined jacket.

"Five!" called another, waving her bidding paddle.

"Six, and I want him to wear that tux on the date!" added someone else from the back.

"For seven thousand, he'll even *dry clean* it first," the emcee joked.

I tried to remind myself that this was all for the charity, that Bright Futures would benefit from every dollar. But, as the price reached nine thousand dollars, the thought of someone else winning a date with Topher was almost too much.

Then a woman whispered something into the emcee's ear, and his voice took on a dramatic tone. "Ladies and gentlemen, hold onto your seats! We have a bid from a mystery guest calling in from New York!

And let me tell you, folks, they are serious about winning this date with Topher Brodie!"

My stomach dropped, and the hurt I'd been trying to hold back surged up all at once. A mystery guest from New York? It didn't take much imagination to guess who that might be. Probably one of those actresses or models he'd been linked to in the tabloids, someone effortlessly glamorous, someone who belonged in his world.

"Fifty thousand dollars!" The emcee's voice boomed again. The crowd collectively gasped, a ripple of shock and excitement filling the room, followed by a thunderous round of applause. "Going once... going twice... and *sold* to our New York bidder for a record-breaking donation."

The emcee clapped along with the audience, practically bouncing with excitement, while Topher gave a modest nod, his expression unreadable as he stepped off the stage. He didn't look for me as he walked back into the crowd.

Instead, he pulled out his phone, answering a call with a curt nod, murmuring something I couldn't hear. He glanced at his watch, his brow furrowing as he continued speaking, completely absorbed, as if he had already forgotten he'd just auctioned himself off for fifty thousand dollars.

My cheeks burned with a mix of anger and humiliation. I'd dressed up, came here, let myself hope. And he had auctioned himself off for a date right in front of me.

I set my glass down, taking one last look at the glittering room before making my way to the exit. As I stepped outside, the cool air hit my face, and I took a deep, steadying breath, the weight of everything pressing down on me.

It was time for me to let go of Topher Brodie and move on.

26

I GRIPPED THE STEERING WHEEL, staring straight ahead, determined to leave the gala—and Topher Brodie—in my rearview mirror for good.

I had the car in reverse, halfway out of my parking spot, when an obnoxiously long black limo inched into view. Slowly. Very slowly.

At first, I waited, assuming the driver would ease past like a normal person.

He did not.

Instead, the limo angled itself across the exit lane and *stopped*, like a five-ton roadblock sent by the universe to ruin my night.

I blinked. "No. Nope. *Absolutely not.*"

I flicked my headlights. Nothing. I tapped the horn. Nothing.

"You've got to be kidding me!" I shouted, leaning out my window. "Move! I don't care how important your passenger is unless it's Beyoncé or the Pope. *MOVE!*"

Still nothing.

Then—*bump.*

A soft jolt rocked my car. I whipped my head forward, mouth dropping open.

"Oh no. Oh *no no no.*" I threw the car in park, flung open the door, and stormed around the front like I was about to personally conduct a citizen's arrest.

"You had ONE JOB!" I shouted at the tinted windshield. "Don't hit parked cars! Are you taking lessons from the *last* limo driver who hit me? Because let me tell you, buddy, I've done this dance before and I swear to all things holy—"

The driver's door opened.

Out stepped Topher.

The very man I had just vowed to forget.

My mouth dropped open, and the words caught somewhere between my brain and my throat. I blinked, half convinced I was imagining him.

"You're driving a limo?" I sputtered, trying to wrap my head around the absurdity of it.

Topher raised his hands, looking somewhere between apologetic and amused. "Well, I wasn't supposed to be. But I saw you leaving, and I had to stop you."

I crossed my arms, dumbfounded. "So let me get this straight— you auctioned yourself off on a date, then *blocked* me in with your limo. And now you're just here, standing in front of my car, like this is normal?"

He winced, but then a slight smile tugged at the corner of his mouth. "Yeah, well, I didn't think it through as clearly as I could have. But if it helps, I brought you something."

I was about to ask what in the world he could have brought that would make any of this better when he reached into his pocket and pulled out something small and familiar, a glint of silver catching the faint parking lot light. I froze, heart stuttering. It was my locket—the tiny silver heart I'd lost months ago, the one that had been my last, most precious link to my parents. I hadn't dared to hope I'd see it again.

My breath caught, and tears pricked my eyes. "How...where... when?" I stammered, reaching out to take it, my fingers brushing the cool metal. I could hardly believe it was real.

Topher gave a small, almost nervous smile, watching my reaction with that soft look in his eyes. "I hired a private investigator. Turns out that your old landlord sold it to a pawn shop. It took some legwork, but my team finally tracked it down and got it back for you." He scratched the back of his neck. "The PI found a few other things too."

"Like what?"

"First, the airport shuttle company? It's under new management. Your old boss Jerry was fired months ago. Turns out there were a lot of complaints against him. You weren't the only one."

"Couldn't have happened to a better man."

"And the limo driver," he went on. "The investigator found a long history of insurance fraud. He filed a claim after the accident, but once they pulled his record, the case was dropped. Apparently, he doesn't need that walker after all, and he has a background of causing accidents."

I threw up my hands. "I *told* you he backed into me! And his knees worked just fine."

"His medical record agrees," Topher said, a half-smile forming. "You were right all along."

I couldn't hold back the tears anymore. I swallowed, gripping the locket tightly in my hand. The weight of it and its history came flooding back. How my parents had given it to me on my sixteenth birthday, how it had traveled with me through every move. Losing it had felt like losing them all over again.

My heart swelled, and a tear slipped down my cheek. "You went to all that trouble just to get this back for me?"

Topher let out a quiet breath. "I knew what it meant to you. I couldn't stand the thought of you being without it. I wanted you to know that someone else cares about the things you care about."

I looked up at Topher, emotions I couldn't control spilling onto my face. "Thank you. I—I thought I'd never see this again."

He seemed to read my expression and offered a small, apologetic smile. "You have no idea how hard it was not to go over to you the second I saw you tonight." His voice was soft, almost shy. "But I wanted to have this in hand first."

"So you ignored me because of this?"

"I had an assistant bring it at the last minute. It was a bit of an undercover operation. I didn't want to risk seeing you and not being able to give you this."

I clutched the locket tighter, feeling the flood of gratitude and something deeper I hadn't let myself feel before. "I read about your donation to Bright Futures."

He glanced down at his hands. "You know, meeting you changed a lot for me. I didn't realize just how much until you were gone." He swallowed, as if the words were hard to say, but he kept going, his gaze meeting mine. "I thought I had everything figured out—business, life, the way I wanted to be seen. But when you showed me Bright Futures, when you spoke about the chance you wanted to give people, it got to me."

My heart was pounding as I watched him, listening to every word. He went on, his voice low. "After you left, I couldn't shake it. I decided to donate to Bright Futures in the way you would have wanted me to. Not because of some tax write-off or for the headlines, but because it was the right thing to do for all the kids who grew up like me. I forgot what it was like, and you made me see what I'd lost along the way."

I blinked, tears welling up again. "Your mom told me about what you did for me by paying off my debt. She said that cost you the company, that your partners used it to force you out."

Topher gave a short nod, a resigned look crossing his face. "They did. Apparently, they'd been looking for an excuse. Helping you was exactly what they needed to justify it. But honestly..." He paused, a small, almost relieved smile flickering across his face. "It was worth it. If that's what it took to look at myself and see how far I'd strayed from the person I wanted to be. The company wasn't worth holding onto."

I shook my head in disbelief. "Topher, that's your *company*. That's everything you built."

"It was. But somewhere along the way, I stopped recognizing the person I'd become. I built it to help people and make something of myself, but I got so caught up in the game that I lost sight of what truly matters. Meeting you reminded me of who I used to be, what I used to care about. And I couldn't live with myself if I didn't do something you would be proud of."

I took a deep, steadying breath. "I'm happy for you."

Topher's gaze softened as he looked at me, his voice low and warm. "You look beautiful, of course. But how are things with you?"

"I'm really happy," I said, the words tumbling out almost as if I had to remind myself it was true. "I wake up in the mornings, and I'm excited again. I didn't even know how much I'd missed that feeling, the feeling that my life could actually go somewhere." I shook my head, a smile breaking through. "I used to think everything was just survival. Like I was just trying to stay afloat. But now, I feel like I'm finally getting to live."

Topher squeezed my hand gently, sending butterflies flitting through my belly. "I'm so glad. I can't even tell you how good it is to hear that." His eyes searched my face. "Where did this new chapter start? How did it all happen?"

A slow smile crept across my face. "Tulane. I enrolled." I spoke with a mix of excitement and disbelief. "I'm studying social work. And it's not just the classes. It's everything. I'm part of a community now, surrounded by people who want to make a difference and who care about the same things I do. It's been amazing. I finally feel like I'm doing something that matters."

His eyes widened, lighting up with pride. "That's incredible. I can already picture you helping people, making a real difference." He took a small step closer, his gaze unwavering.

My heart swelled, and a shy, almost disbelieving smile crept onto my face. This was the moment I'd imagined a dozen different ways, and somehow, it was even better than I'd dreamed. But then a thought flickered through my mind, uninvited and sharp, cutting through my happiness.

A hint of disappointment tugged at me as I thought of that fifty-thousand-dollar bid from the mysterious New York caller. My stomach twisted a little, the warmth of the moment dimming as I thought of him with some glamorous model or actress, some effortlessly perfect woman who belonged in his world far more than I did.

Topher must have seen the change in my face because he tilted his head, a small crease of concern in his brow. "What's wrong?"

I forced a laugh, trying to shake off the feeling. "The fifty-thousand-dollar date." I looked away, trying to sound casual, even though my voice wavered slightly. "Whoever she is, I'm sure she's thrilled to have won it."

Topher's face softened, and a smirk tugged at the corner of his mouth. "Oh, that date," he murmured, his tone playful.

I raised an eyebrow, confused. "Yes, *that* date." That might have come out a little sharper than I'd intended. "I mean, I'm sure whoever paid fifty thousand dollars is expecting a lot from Mr. Topher Brodie."

He chuckled softly, taking another step toward me, his voice low and earnest. "You're right. But here's the thing. I paid that fifty thousand dollars myself."

I blinked, processing his words, my heart doing a ridiculous little flip. "Wait, *you* bought the date?"

He nodded, his expression mischievous. "Exactly. There's only one person I want to go on that date with." He leaned in, a warm smile playing on his lips, and brushed a strand of hair back from my cheek, his fingers lingering as if he couldn't quite bring himself to let go. "You."

My heart skipped as warmth flooded my cheeks.

"That is," he said, "if you'll go with me, Kathleen. Will you?"

I tried to play it cool, but the smile creeping onto my face betrayed me. "I guess if someone's willing to spend fifty thousand dollars on a date..." I paused, letting him hang on my answer. "How could I say no?"

His smile widened, relief and excitement flashing in his eyes. He took my hand in his, giving it a gentle squeeze. "Good. Because I've got big plans, Ms. Avery."

My breath hitched, and the world faded around us as he leaned in, closing the last of the distance between us. His lips brushed mine softly at first, gentle and tentative, as if he was savoring the moment as much as I was. But then the kiss deepened, warmth spreading through me, making everything else—every doubt, every past hurt—fall away.

We pulled back slowly, both of us breathless, his hand still cradling my face. He looked at me with that familiar sparkle in his eyes, now mixed with something more vulnerable.

I couldn't help but grin, shaking my head in disbelief. "Alright, so tell me," I teased, arching an eyebrow, "what exactly does a fifty-thousand-dollar date look like? I mean, the bar's pretty high after that swan-boat extravaganza you planned."

He placed a hand over his heart, looking mock-offended. "Are you doubting my ability to sweep you off your feet?"

"Oh, not at all," I shot back with a grin. "I'm just making sure you get your money's worth."

He grinned, pulling me close, his tone softening as he looked into my eyes. "Whatever it is, I promise, it'll be unforgettable. This is just the beginning."

EPILOGUE

ONE YEAR LATER

IT TURNS out fifty thousand dollars buys you a truly unforgettable date—or at least an unforgettable redo.

Topher had insisted on planning our long-promised "fifty-thousand-dollar date" to celebrate my Tulane graduation. So, when we pulled up to the lake near City Park and I saw a row of swan boats bobbing on the water, all decked out with twinkling lights and tiny bouquets tied to the bows, I burst out laughing.

"You really went all out," I teased, glancing over at him.

Topher grinned, reaching out a hand to help me into one of the boats, then sliding in next to me. "I figured our last swan boat experience was a little lacking."

"Lacking?" I laughed. "We nearly capsized!"

He chuckled, easing us out onto the water as a gentle breeze caught the lights, sending shimmering reflections dancing across the lake. "This time, no near-death experiences. I promise."

We drifted under the soft glow of lanterns strung along the lake's edge, and it felt both absurd and perfect—so very *us* in every way.

"So," I said with a playful smile, "this is what a fifty-thousand-dollar date looks like?"

He leaned back, giving me a smirk. "Romantic, right? I mean, it took a year to pull it off, but I think I finally nailed it."

He'd nailed everything he'd done as my boyfriend in the last year. I'd never doubted he would get this right, too.

I squeezed his hand, grinning. "Now I get to say I've been on two swan boat dates with you, which has to be some kind of record." He hung his head, hiding a small smile, and I nudged my elbow into his ribs. "Another record—how quickly you've launched your new company, Topher. I'm proud of you."

He chuckled, then glanced around. "Turns out helping people out of debt is a little harder than renting swan boats."

"You seem to be managing all right." After being kicked out of the company he founded, Topher turned right around and worked to help transform the industry, giving aid to the people who had been hurt by his lending practices. He started a profitable business focused on helping people overwhelmed by debt, like my parents and his mom had been. He was still relentless, still a workaholic, but now his work was as meaningful as it was successful. And, somehow, he still found time for *us*.

He gave me a soft look. "What about you? The amazing work you're doing with your kids?"

I smiled, thinking of the young people I was helping as a newly graduated social worker. "It's intense but rewarding, helping them process their grief and find a sense of stability. So many of them are going through what I did, trying to understand why life can change so quickly when a parent dies, but I can see them starting to heal. I finally feel like I'm doing what I was meant to do."

Now, as we planned the next holiday season together, we were already scheming to deck out Josephine's tiny house with more lights and garland than it could handle. She'd made it very clear she wasn't moving out anytime soon. At least not until, as she'd hinted, there were grandchildren.

As we drifted on the lake, watching the twinkling lights reflect off the water, I looked around the swan boat, grinning. "So, tell me, how exactly does one even *try* to spend fifty grand on a swan boat date?"

Topher smirked, leaning back with a faux-serious look. "Oh, I'll have you know, it wasn't easy."

I glanced around. "You didn't... buy these swan boats, did you?"

"Tempting, but no," he said, shaking his head. "The swan boats remain available to the public. Although I did think about it."

I snorted. "So what, you bought the lake?"

"It's a public lake!" He clicked his tongue against the roof of his mouth. "I don't think they're selling it."

"Then what *did* you buy?" I squinted suspiciously.

He grinned. "Oh, just a little something to make this date truly unforgettable."

Just then, a man in a rowboat paddled over and handed Topher a small picnic basket.

I raised an eyebrow. "Topher, we already ate. What's in here?"

He gave me a mischievous smile, holding the basket up as if it were the crown jewels. "Let's just say this time, we're keeping everything well above the waterline. No near-capsizing incidents."

"Good call," I said, laughing.

He grinned wider, leaning closer. "Trust me, this is one swan boat date you'll never forget."

He handed the basket to me. I peeked inside, and my heart skipped a beat. Nestled among folded linen napkins was a small velvet box.

I looked up at him, eyes wide. He smiled, holding the box out for me. "Kathleen," he murmured. "I've realized that there's nothing in the world—no amount of success, no sum of money, nothing—that compares to what I feel when I'm with you."

He took a breath, his gaze meeting mine. "I spent years chasing something I couldn't even define, thinking that if I just achieved one more thing, or pushed a little harder, I'd be happy. But I was wrong.

Happiness wasn't in any of those things. It was here with you, and I didn't even know it until I almost lost you."

My throat tightened as he continued.

"You're the reason I want to be a better man. You remind me of the person I want to be. And I want to spend my life making you happy, loving you, and sharing all the ridiculous swan-boat dates we can handle."

He opened the box, revealing a beautiful, sparkling ring.

Topher took a deep breath, then glanced down at the limited space around him, clearly determined. He tried to maneuver himself onto one knee, but the swan boat wobbled ominously, tipping slightly to one side.

"Oh no, what are you doing?" I asked, as he grabbed the edge of the boat for balance.

He gripped the seat with one hand and clutched the ring box with the other, his face a mix of love and panic. "I didn't factor in the whole... capsizing hazard."

"Maybe stay seated?" I suggested, laughing. "I'd hate for your proposal to end with us swimming to shore."

He chuckled, staying firmly on both knees and extending the ring. "Good idea." As he looked up at me, his eyes softened. "So, without capsizing... will you marry me?"

Tears filled my eyes as I looked from the ring to his face, stunned and overjoyed all at once. "Yes," I whispered, nodding as he slipped the ring onto my finger.

Topher smiled, pulling me close, and as our lips met, the world around us faded, leaving only the two of us on that softly glowing lake.

This was real. It was finally, beautifully, real. And it was forever.

THE END

ALSO BY THE AUTHOR

Celebrity Love in New Orleans (complete series)

Scandalously Yours
Starfully Yours
Suddenly Yours
Secretly Yours
Suitably Yours (novella)

Thank You

In love with New Orleans? Go to my website at www.katietalbotau-thor.com, and sign up for my newsletter to get a free novella, Suit-ably Yours.

ABOUT THE AUTHOR

Katie Talbot writes romantic comedies about sassy, smart heroines. Her debut five-book series, *Celebrity Love in New Orleans,* is set in the city she calls home. Originally from Nebraska, she now lives in the Big Easy with her husband and three wonderful children.

ACKNOWLEDGMENTS

I would like to thank my parents, who fostered my love of writing throughout the years. For pretending you couldn't see me reading under the covers with a flashlight every night before bed. It's hard to imagine anyone having more books in their family home, and that was a wonderful way to grow up.

Thank you to my children—P, L, and MV. And to P, thank you for being my biggest fan.

Thank you to my brothers and sisters-in-law and my nieces and nephews, for being early and enthusiastic supporters.

To my writing group, Amy Page, KC Newbury, and Elyse Haynes, who have been instrumental every step of the way. You all have helped me so much along the way, including brainstorming the meet cute in this novel, which lit a fire under me to keep writing.

To my editor, Whitney Jones of Empowered Writing, who coached me for this novel. It wouldn't have happened without you.

And to my readers: I hope you like the story of Topher and Kathleen as much as I enjoyed writing it.

Stay smart, stay sassy,

Katie

www.ingramcontent.com/pod-product-compliance
Lightning Source LLC
Chambersburg PA
CBHW050838180626
46814CB00007B/2513